RULES FOR DATING YOUR EX

PIPER RAYNE

This book is a work of fiction. Names, characters, places and incidents either are products of the author's imagination or are used fictitiously. Any resemblance to actual events or locales or persons, living or dead, is entirely coincidental.

© 2020 by Piper Rayne

All rights reserved, including the right to reproduce this book or portions thereof in any form whatsoever.

Cover Design: By Hang Le

1st Line Editor: Joy Editing

2nd Line Editor: My Brother's Editor

Proofreader: Shawna Gavas, Behind The Writer

ABOUT RULES FOR DATING YOUR EX

If your ex arrives in your hometown eighteen months after you walked out on him while you were eight months pregnant, follow this short list of rules before you give him a second chance.

Rule #1 – Don't stand in the way of your brothers who want to rough him up.
Rule #2 – Don't meet him for coffee and agree to allow him to meet your daughter.
Rule #3 – Don't drool when your daughter falls asleep on his chest for the first time. It's just your ovaries talking.
Rule #4 – Don't let him hold your hand. While we're at it, no hugs, no kisses on the cheek… just no physical contact in general. That only leads to remembering better times.

The last one is the most important…

Rule #5 – When you find yourself needing someone's help and you're tired of always asking your family, don't let him be the one who's there for you.

Because all those good qualities of his will suck you right back in and you'll have no chance of fighting your feelings, especially now that he's ready to be a father to your daughter.

Rules for *Dating Your Ex*

The Baileys

Austin Bailey - 38 years old
(*Biology Teacher/Baseball Coach*)
Savannah Bailey - 36 years old
(*Runs Bailey Timber Corp*)
Brooklyn Bailey - 33 years old
(*Runs Essential Oil Company*)
Rome Bailey - 31 years old
(*Chef*)
Denver Bailey - 31 years old
(*Bush Pilot*)
Juno Bailey - 30 years old
(*Matchmaker*)
Kingston Bailey - 27 years old
(*Smokejumper*)
Phoenix Bailey - 25 years old
(*Singer*)
Sedona Bailey - 25 years old
(*Travel Writer*)

ONE

Sedona

A soft, warm breeze flows into the restaurant when the door opens, and all the guests turn toward the door to see who's arrived. Jamison stands with his suitcase next to him, gaze scouring the space as though he didn't just walk into a Bailey baby shower. My breath seizes and my throat closes up for a second before I react.

I shift eighteen-month-old Palmer behind me. She squirms, but my grip only grows tighter to keep her hidden in place. She hits my thighs, whining and not understanding, but I don't budge. You'd think we were being held at gunpoint from the way my heart races and sweat beads along my back. My mama bear instinct has kicked in and it's fierce. My free hand covers my swollen belly, his eyes follow my movement and his face drains of color.

My brothers and brothers-in-law line up shoulder to shoulder in front of the rest of us. Kingston's in the middle, arms across his chest. He's the most protective since he's been playing the part of Palmer's pseudo dad for the past eighteen months. She tried to call him daddy last week, and I had to have the conversation about how he's her uncle, not her daddy. Thankfully, she got distracted and didn't ask any other questions. I'll never allow her to not know the truth of who her father is, but she's too young to understand.

Then again, I never thought he'd be standing in front of me right now. I imagined that when we came face to face again, I'd have my life in order. I'd have my travel blog up and running, not still doing freelance work. I wanted to have my own house, not be living in my brother's apartment. I wanted to be stunning and gorgeous, not thirty pounds heavier with swollen ankles and fingers that look like sausages. The only real physical asset on me right now is my breasts that have doubled in size.

"Hey, King," Jamison says in his Scottish brogue. He'd lost a lot of his accent after living in America for so long, but it's still there.

Half the guests gasp—I assume over the fact that he used my brother's nickname. My brother's wife Cleo reaches out and squeezes my shoulder.

Kingston's stance widens, and Palmer continues to hit my thighs. I loosen my grip on her and she slides between my legs, running forward. I reach for her, but she wiggles out of her yellow cardigan and out of my hold.

Phoenix snatches her before she can break past the wall of testosterone, but Palmer kicks and throws her tiny fists at her aunt, whining and screeching. Phoenix glances at me, silently asking what I want her to do. I nod for her to let my daughter go. Let the bastard see her. See what he gave up.

Phoenix lowers Palmer's feet to the floor as my entire family watches with rapt attention. I know my daughter and who she'll go to, and I trust that he'll protect her.

As I assumed, Palmer snakes around Kingston's leg,

peeking out from behind him. His hand comes down on her head as he looks over his shoulder at me, probably wondering why I'd allow this. But I nod. Jamison's here. He'll see her at some point, and it's better for me to have my family supporting me when it happens.

Kingston scoops Palmer up in his muscular arms.

She signs to him. *Who?*

King looks to me for an answer, and I shake my head. So Kingston signs back. *Nobody.*

Palmer's curiosity isn't satisfied though. *Why here?*

Kingston blows out a breath, not happy to be in the situation I've put him in. This is my responsibility, not my big brother's, so I step forward, but Phoenix's hand clamps down on my wrist. I shake it off and go around my brothers' defensive line. I guess I know where Palmer gets her unwillingness to listen.

"Don't, Sedona," Denver says in a soft tone.

I hold up my hand. "I have no choice. He's here."

We talk about Jamison as though he's not right in front of us. His eyes haven't left my stomach yet. Not even to look at the little girl in Kingston's arms. The ironic thing is that I look much the same as I did the day I walked out on him. He had passed out on the couch, and like some sad movie character with my suitcase in hand, I gave him one last glance before shutting the door on that chapter of my life.

"Sedona," Kingston says, and I turn.

Palmer signs at me. *Mommy. Mommy.*

I hold up my finger to her. When I turn back to Jamison, grabbing him by the arm to drag him outside, his eyes are locked on Palmer, his feet planted firm.

My heart gallops like a wild horse racing through the wilderness. I want to run over to Kingston, snatch Palmer out of his arms, and run away as fast and far as I can.

Granted, that wouldn't be fast or far with how pregnant I am, but still.

Tears fill Jamison's eyes, and I look back at Palmer, who's now fixated on her father. She's too young to see what the rest of us do. Their shared blue eyes. Their same thin nose and thick wavy hair. Although her hair is darker than his, resembling more my shade, no one could deny she's his. And there's no doubt, with his full attention on her, he's put it all together.

If he's drunk like he was when I left him, he could think he's warped back to eighteen months ago and I'm still carrying his baby.

He takes his hand off the suitcase he wheeled in and lifts both hands. Palmer focuses on him as if she's watching the Lake Starlight baseball team. My girl loves baseball, something her uncles couldn't be happier about. Maybe I'm wrong. Maybe she sees the resemblance, even at her young age.

Jamison signs to her. *Hello. Nice to meet you.*

My head whips to Palmer as she smiles, signing back. *Hello.*

Oh hell no. I grab Jamison's arm again, pulling him out of Terra and Mare.

He follows without a fight this time, and I release him as soon as we reach the sidewalk. But seeing all the faces of my family plastered to the windows, I grab him again and move us farther down the sidewalk and out of everyone's sight.

"Yer pregnant?" he asks.

"That's obvious. What are you doing here?"

Now that the immediate threat to Palmer is gone, my gaze skates across him. I hate that my body isn't listening to my brain. He looks good, healthy—and resembles the guy I fell in love with, not the guy I left. His cheeks are rosy, his body lean with muscle. His bright blue eyes sparkle, no longer dull and glazed over as they had been for so long.

Our eyes catch as though we both took a trip down memory lane, except I definitely don't resemble the woman he fell in love with. I'm far from that seventeen-year-old girl he'd flirt with in the hallway of our high school.

"I'm here for you and our daughter." He says it as though he can snap his fingers and we'll grab our bags and be off. But that's Jamison's way. He got everything he ever wanted until he didn't. And then he decided to destroy his life.

I cross my arms and his eyes dip to my cleavage. He probably forgot how big my breasts got with Palmer because a bottle of vodka was more appealing than I was in those days. "Sorry, we're not available."

"I'm clean," he rushes out. "For a year."

"Good. I'm happy for you." It's true. I might not love Jamison anymore, but one day, Palmer will want answers and I'd like to tell her that her father got his shit together.

"I never should have let you leave."

A huff escapes me. "Hard to fight for us when you're passed out. I was always curious how many days it took you to realize I'd left you."

He looks dazed, as if he doesn't remember. Probably kept waking up and thinking I was at the store. "I want a second chance."

I shake my head.

"Is she deaf?" he asks, changing the course of our conversation.

But I want to keep all things Palmer away from him until I have a better idea what's going on with him these days. "Listen, I'm in the middle of something. Are you staying at Glacier Point?"

If he is, I'll be pissed at my brother-in-law Wyatt for not giving me a heads-up that my ex booked a room.

"Um, I haven't booked a room anywhere yet. I just flew in this morning."

"So you were just going to wheel your suitcase around and hope you found me?" Typical unprepared Jamison.

"I wasn't sure. I've been planning this moment for so many months, and now that I'm here, so close to you, I didn't know what to do. My plan went out the window. Yer gorgeous, by the way, but you were when you were pregnant with our daughter too."

He reaches out to touch me, and I retract my arm. "Funny, I never thought you noticed."

His head tilts, and he tries to use that same look that would get me to forget our stupid fights back when we were together. Well, not this time. This isn't him leaving the toilet seat up or not loading the dishwasher.

"I've loved you since I've known you. Of course I noticed you. You glowed just like you do now. But tell me, do I have competition? Who's the father of your baby?" He glances at my left hand and I pull it behind my back.

A million lies flash through my brain like comic-strip thought bubbles above my head. My ring doesn't fit anymore, so I took it off. We're not engaged… yet. But all of it is a lie, so I go with snark. "My life is none of your business."

He nods. "Just hear me out. One coffee or tea or whatever you can drink in your condition."

I roll my eyes. "I'm happy you're doing well, but nothing is going to change between the two of us."

His shoulders slump, and he says nothing for a minute. "Just one coffee. I understand yer mad, I would be too, but I'm only asking for you to hear me out."

I fight the impulse to say yes. He was always hard to say no to, hence how I ended up pregnant. "I don't know. It's been a long time."

"Please, Sedona. Please." A line forms at the bridge of his nose as he pleads with me.

The door of Terra and Mare opens, and we glance over to find Kingston wheeling out Jamison's suitcase and resting it by the side of the building. Instead of going back inside, he stands there with his arms crossed, staring at us.

"King," I say with an irritated tone.

"It's just such a beautiful day. I want to take full advantage." He shoves his hands in his pockets and his head circles up to stare at the sky.

The door opens again a second later and Stella shoots me a sympathetic look while trying to drag Kingston back inside the restaurant. They exchange a few words, but Stella wins per usual.

Once they're gone, I say to Jamison, "Now is not the time. I have to get back in there."

He nods. "Tomorrow?"

I exhale a big breath. "I don't know."

"Please?"

I guess I wouldn't mind some explanations after all this time. Plus, it gives me an opportunity to tell him it's completely over between us since he seems to be on a mission to win me back—if what he says can be believed. "Fine."

He reaches out again and I step back. His hands fall to his side. "Thank you."

"But not here." I glance around. "I've kept us out of Buzz Wheel for this long, and I don't want that changing. A lot of people still know you here. Meet me in Sunrise Bay.

Tomorrow at ten o'clock. There's a diner called Two Brothers and an Egg."

"Perfect. I'll be there." He smiles and I ignore the way it chips at my defenses.

I nod and walk back toward the entrance to Terra and Mare.

"Sedona?"

I circle back to face him.

"Is she deaf?"

I nod and move to open the door, but my curiosity gets the better of me. "How do you know how to sign?"

"My uncle was deaf."

So there's the answer to the question about Palmer's deafness.

He must see me trying to remember ever meeting his uncle because he says, "He died when I was over here during senior year, remember?"

Vaguely, but we had so much going on, and we were trying to figure out how we would stay together after high school ended. Though now that I'm thinking about it, all I remember is him not going home for the funeral because his family couldn't afford the airfare.

"Bye, Jamison," I say.

He raises his hand. "I'll see you tomorrow."

I open the door and disappear into Terra and Mare, taking my seat.

Palmer slides off of Stella's lap and climbs onto mine. The one thing I miss most now that I'm so pregnant is that I can't get her as close as I want when I hug her. She nuzzles in my arms and rests her head on my belly because it's her nap time.

Phoenix sits next to me and grabs my hand, conveying that we'll get through this. I know she believes that. I run my free hand through Palmer's hair and watch her breathing become shallower and shallower as she drifts off to sleep.

Oh, baby girl, our world just blew up and you don't even know it. But rest assured, I'll never allow him to hurt her the way he's hurt me. That's a promise.

TWO

Jamison

My heart lurches watching Sedona walk back into the restaurant, knowing our daughter is in there. I'd do just about anything to turn back time and change what I did to make me lose everything I care about.

I dial my sponsor, Merrick, on my phone.

"How did it go?" he says.

"She's agreed to coffee tomorrow."

"Good. That's good. And how do you feel?"

I've already talked to Merrick three times today. At the airport, after my flight landed, and right before I walked into the Baileys' den, Terra and Mare. I took a chance that I'd find them there when I saw Kingston walk into the restaurant hand in hand with Stella. I was surprised, though not shocked to see those two together as a couple but figured they might lead me to more Baileys. Turns out I was right. But I didn't think I'd be walking into a baby shower. Nor did I anticipate that it would be Sedona's.

She's blocked me from all social media since she split.

"Jamie?" Merrick says.

"Sorry. Yeah, I'm here. No urges I can't handle or anything."

"We talked about this. It's not an easy fix. She's not going to run back into your arms. You have to do the work to get the prize."

I nod. Everything he's saying is true, but I hate being on the wrong side of that door. "She's deaf."

"Sedona?"

"My daughter," I say, my voice catching. I sit on a park bench, conjuring up her sweet little face in my mind. "She's adorable. Has my eyes but Sedona's hair. And she has no fucking clue who I am." I lean forward, my elbows rest on my knees.

"What's her name?"

I shake my head. "I have no idea."

"But you know she's deaf?" Merrick asks.

"She signed to me." The memory of Kingston signing that I was "nobody" when she asked who I was flashes through my mind. That was like the quick flick of a sword across my heart.

"That's awesome. You can sign?" He sounds surprised.

"I'm rusty, but yeah, my uncle was deaf."

I grew up watching my cousins and parents sign with my uncle, and I guess you pick it up quickly when you're a kid. It was only when I got older that I realized we didn't sign like anyone else I knew. My mother eventually explained that my uncle had learned how to sign when he lived in the United States with an old family friend. Apparently American Sign Language is different from British Sign Language. I never thought I'd be so grateful for something that had left my uncle so isolated in Scotland.

I wonder what my mom will say when I tell her. But at

this point, she doesn't even know I have a daughter, let alone a deaf daughter. I'm not ready for how disappointed she'll sound when she finds out my behavior chased off my family just yet.

"That's an upside—a barrier you don't' have to worry about. You won't have to learn to communicate with her."

Merrick always sees the bright side of everything. I guess it's his job, as my sponsor, to put a positive spin on things, but it can be annoying as fuck sometimes too.

"Yeah, I guess. But it hurts, you know. I'm the reason I'm not in my baby girl's life. I did this."

"You put yourself in this position, that's true. But you have to forgive yourself. I've already told you my worries about you going out there. You can't make Sedona forgive you. It's her choice whether she wants to or not, but you have to remember that whatever she chooses, doesn't speak to who you are now."

"Gotcha."

We've been over this. It's why I waited a year after getting clean to contact her—to make sure it wouldn't be for naught. The worst thing that could happen is that Sedona forgives me and then I relapse and all that mistrust piles up again. I wouldn't get a third chance. But waiting a whole year, especially the first six months after rehab and the halfway house, was excruciating.

Now that I've seen them, it's all so real. The hurt in her eyes, the fear when she saw me looking at our daughter... I'm not sure she'll ever forgive me.

"Just go find a hotel and get yourself together for coffee tomorrow. Hopefully the two of you can find some common ground. Remember that Sedona has the right to feel however she wants, but if you want a relationship with your daughter, you can have that without Sedona. You have rights as a father."

"A father who's been absent her entire life," I grumble.

"A father who was getting clean to be the best damn father he could be. A court will see that. You have rights and don't forget that."

"You talk from experience?"

His laugh is hollow. "I do."

He doesn't give me anything else, so I don't press him. "Okay, I'm going to find a hotel. Thanks for talking to me."

"You don't have to thank me. I'm here for you whenever, day or night. I can't stress enough that there's no quick fix to this. You have to do the work, just like you did to get clean."

"I know. I know. Thanks."

We hang up and I hold the phone for a moment before ordering an Uber to Glacier Point Resort.

Fifteen minutes later, the Uber picks me up and we drive past Terra and Mare, the windows revealing everyone having a great time inside. I close my eyes briefly. My family is in there.

"I'm going to win you over," I whisper.

"What's that?" the Uber driver asks.

I shake my head in the rearview mirror. "Nothing."

We ride in silence to the resort while I pray that I'm not blacklisted from everywhere in this town.

THE NEXT MORNING, I'm walking through the lobby of the resort when a big body makes its way over to me from the reception office. I stop, figuring he'd catch up with me at some point, but I'm surprised by his tentative smile.

"Jamison," Wyatt says.

"Mornin', Wyatt."

He crosses his arms and widens his stance. "You know I can't let you stay here, right? My wife will kick my ass."

"I'm a paying customer."

His lips don't tilt up. He merely nods. "You won't be after today. I can't have you here."

"Listen, I'm having breakfast with Sedona." I glance at my watch and Wyatt's eyes fall to my Patek Philippe watch with raised eyebrows. "I can't be late, so I'll have to check out as soon as I get back. It'll be a bit late, but I had planned on staying another few nights. That work for you?"

"Fine. But you really should've brought a bodyguard back with you."

He turns on his heel and stops to speak to the receptionist. After a moment, both their gazes fall to me. Great, I guess I really am finding somewhere else to put me up.

I hop in my Uber, driven by Duke Thompson. Perfect. He'll probably drop me off in some remote part of Alaska and I'll be eaten by a Kodiak bear, much to the Bailey family's satisfaction.

He recognizes me, turning around and shaking my hand. "Jamison, I heard something about you being in town."

I want to say no shit, Buzz Wheel outed me last night. I read the article, which didn't portray me in a very flattering light. The first time I have an article centered around me in that gossip rag and I'm a deadbeat father. "I need to go to Sunrise Bay. Two Brothers and an Egg restaurant?"

He nods, puts the car in drive, and we pull away from the resort.

After I give him enough one-word answers, Duke finally stops asking me questions. The closer we get to

Sunrise Bay, the more my stomach tightens. This moment reminds me of the same feeling I used to get when I was taking a penalty shot on the pitch. It all comes down to this. This is my only shot to try to get her to listen to me.

Things with Sedona were always easy. Maybe not entirely or we wouldn't be in the situation we are. But we fell in love fast at seventeen when everyone thought it was infatuation more than love. Even when I was playing in Europe and she was at school in New York, she'd message me to say, "great goal" or "congratulations on the win." When she got on the college newspaper, I subscribed and read every word she ever wrote. I missed her beyond all reason. That's why when I got offered a spot in the MLS— to play for New York, no less—I was on her doorstep right after the plane landed. It's always been Sedona for me.

"We're here," Duke interrupts my thoughts.

I blink, shifting my gaze to him, surprised we're here already. Sedona's at a booth inside along the window. She's smiling at the waiter in front of her table with a pad of paper. She signals to the empty side of the booth and he nods, moving on to the next table.

"Wish me luck, Duke." I climb out of his car, mustering all the confidence I can to meet this head-on. Own up to my mistakes and beg for forgiveness.

The bell on the door rings when I walk through, and her gaze shoots up to meet mine. Her smile from a second ago turns to a scowl. Her hair is up in a ponytail, exposing one of my favorite body parts of her body. Did she do that on purpose to torment me? But I shake it off. Sedona doesn't play like that.

She turns her attention out the window and the scorned feeling inside me knows I don't deserve her full attention. I'm not worthy of those brown eyes scanning my body the way they used to—like she couldn't get enough of me. She never gave me hell about my workout regimen and would praise my abs, biceps, and how strong my thighs were. I'm still fit, but I don't work out like a professional athlete anymore.

I slide into the booth and she rests her hands on her swollen tummy, forcing her gaze back my way.

"Good mornin'," I say.

"Morning."

"You look beautiful."

She rolls her eyes. "Don't."

"What? I can't be honest?"

An annoyed breath falls from her lips. "Let's just get this over with. What do you want?"

"Want?" My forehead creases.

"I have all the money you've sent." She pulls out a check from her purse and slides it over to me.

A big burly guy comes over. A different one than Sedona was talking to before. "What will it be for you two?"

"Just hot water and honey, thanks. I have my own tea bag."

"And you?" he asks me.

I eye his name tag. Tad. Interesting. "Coffee and an egg white omelet with peppers and mushrooms." I put the menu I never looked at back behind the salt and pepper shakers.

He taps the tip of his pen on the notepad and smiles. "Be up soon."

Once he walks away, I stare at the check and calculate the math. Sure enough, it tallies to almost the same amount I've paid her since our daughter was born. I push the check back toward her. "I don't want the money back. That's for you and her."

"I didn't spend a dime of it. I put it in an account for Pa—her." She almost told me our precious little girl's name.

"What's her name?"

She tilts her head and tortures me for another second, looking conflicted. "Palmer."

I nod.

She scowls. "What? You don't like it?"

I raise my hands. "I like it."

"Well, I couldn't very well wait until her father decided to show up so he could have a say."

Our eyes lock, and all that animosity alive and growing inside her reflects back at me. I realize how right Merrick was—I should be praying for a damn miracle, because Sedona will never take me back.

THREE

Sedona

The owner brings us our drinks and I use the interruption to study Jamison further. The only logical explanation for me finding Jamison so damn attractive is that I'm pregnant and overflowing with hormones. It's certainly not normal to want to nail someone on a diner table during the breakfast rush when you hate said person. And hate is a polite way of labeling my feelings for Jamison.

He's not as cut as he was when we were together, but he's still fit. The athletic body he loved to show off could be hiding under his jeans and long-sleeve Henley, but you didn't need X-ray vision back in the day to know he had a body of steel.

"I love her name. And I'd never expect you to wait."

I nod, sipping my tea. I told myself I would be an adult about this.

"Are you playing?" I ask to steer the conversation away from Palmer.

He shakes his head with a disappointed glint in his eye.

"I guess you don't follow me anymore." He stares at his coffee, then glances up.

I ignore the pull to tell him I know everything the tabloids have said about him. Everything from his rock bottom to rehab to a halfway house. I chased down every rumor that he was dating someone. Hell, I've probably kept better track of him than the FBI could.

"My career is over."

"I'm sorry," I say, and he nods.

I remember when I heard the news that he wouldn't be coming back from his injury. I thought maybe things could've changed, but I guess not. His dream shattered only a few years after he started really playing. It's so unfair. He shrugs it off, but I watched him chase his dream, saw what he put into making it happen, how hard he worked. Enough to know that inside, it must be killing him, festering and eating him alive.

"What's your plan now?" I ask.

He brings his coffee to his lips. "Not sure. Coaching maybe? But I'm really only concerned about getting you to forgive me right now."

Those blue eyes of his lock with mine, and I tear my gaze away before I accept his apology too quickly. It's not like he's apologizing for stepping on my toe or forgetting to call. *Grab that backbone, Sedona. Phoenix would never let him get away with this, but then again, I've never been like my sister that way.*

"I'm not available."

He eyes my stomach once more as a sour look crosses his face. "I figured as much. Who's the lucky guy?"

"It doesn't matter. I wouldn't go there with you ever again, regardless. Now, if you want to talk Palmer, we can work something out. But me and you are off the table." I waggle my finger back and forth between us.

He leans across the table. "I want to see her. I want to be a part of her life."

I lean back as far as I can in the booth, but my stomach hits the edge of the table. The waiter comes by and slides one plate my way and another in front of Jamison.

"I brought you a muffin and fruit. On the house," the waiter says to me. "I couldn't bear having a pregnant mama in here not eating. No offense."

"Thank you, but we'll happily pay for it," I say before I realize I said we. He smiles and walks away, but I stop him before he gets too far. "I mean *I*. *I* will pay for it."

The waiter glances back at Jamison, then back at me, placing his hand over mine. "On the house. No arguing with the owner." He points.

Sure enough, there's a sign nailed to the wall that says exactly that.

I nod. "Thank you."

"You're welcome."

By the time I turn around, Jamison is almost half done with his omelet. "You always did have yer admirers," he says between swallows.

"That felt like a dig."

"Just a fact," he says, mumbling over his mouth full of food.

"And I wasn't the one with the admirers."

He holds my gaze for longer than is comfortable. "I *never* cheated on you."

I nod. That's not what today is supposed to be about, so I deter the conversation from anything to do with our shared past. "I have some stipulations before I let you meet Palmer."

He pushes away his now empty plate, sips his coffee, wipes his mouth, and grants me his undivided attention. "Non-negotiable?"

"Kind of, yes. This isn't a pet we're sharing. She's a little girl with feelings and a heart that I don't want broken."

He nods. "I'm well aware of that."

Questions and thoughts rush around my head like a swarm of bees—he didn't seem to know those things once upon a time.

"If we do this and you're serious about getting to know her, then you do it with me present. We take this slow. And I'm warning you, Jamison, if you so much as miss one date we make, I'll strip her away from you without blinking. You can haul me into court, and I'll hire the best lawyer. I will not let her get hurt." A laugh bubbles out of him, and I narrow my eyes. I tear off a piece of my muffin. "What could possibly be funny right now?"

"You. The protective mama bear. I like it." His vision dips to my lips and back to my eyes.

I could throw back an insult or two about his absence, but I think about Palmer and when she called Kingston daddy. Her scrunched up little nose when I said he's her uncle, not her daddy. Every one of her cousins has a mom and dad, so of course she assumes she has a daddy too.

I study the man across the table. The sweet boy who never would've abandoned his daughter has to be in there somewhere. Maybe he's here now. Maybe rehab changed him, and he'll be the dad I always thought he'd be.

"What's your schedule like this week?" I ask, trying my hardest to keep the conversation on track.

"I'm wide open. Well, actually I'll be trying to find somewhere to stay this afternoon and I'm going to rent a car, but—"

"Why? Where did you stay last night?" I mentally reprimanded myself for asking. Asking means I care, and I *don't* care.

"I was at Glacier Point, but yer brother-in-law is kicking me out."

I bite the inside of my cheek to keep my smile from forming, but I must suck at it because Jamison shakes his head and smirks.

"Go ahead and be happy. I'm pretty sure I should look here in Sunrise Bay for the time being because no one in Lake Starlight wants to see me."

My heart pinches, damn it. "Maybe that'd be best."

I ignore the sour feeling in my stomach. Pushing my plate to the side, having only eaten a bite of the muffin and nothing else, I shift in my seat to get more comfortable. Pretty much an impossibility.

Jamison eyes the plate and slides it back my way. "You need to eat."

I roll my eyes. "Thanks for the advice, doctor, but I'm fine." I take my phone out of my purse. "Same number?"

He shakes his head and pulls out his phone. "You?"

"Yeah," I say, not allowing myself to focus on the fact that he had my number for more than eighteen months and never used it.

My phone vibrates in my hand. It's a text message of a smiley face from an unknown number. The notification blocks Palmer's face in the picture I snapped last week when she decided to pull out every pot and pan I own.

"That's me," Jamison says.

I put my phone back in my purse. "I'll message you a meeting time. We'll keep it public, so maybe the park or something." Sliding out of the booth, I'm aware of Jamison staring at me. "Goodbye, Jamison." I stand at the edge of the booth. "Please just make sure this is what you want before you meet us. There's no going back once we start this process."

He nods.

I walk away, fully aware I'm not nearly as prepared for this new version of our relationship as I need to be.

PHOENIX SITS on her porch when I pull up to her house. She's basking in the sun with her head facing up. She looks in my direction as I put the car in park. I exit the vehicle and she walks toward me. My mental pep talk from the car ride over about not getting upset crumbles as soon as her arms wrap around me in a tight hug.

"Come on. Griffin took Maverick and Palmer on a bike ride, and I may have called Grandma Dori and informed her where. We have some extra time."

I laugh as she leads me to the front door. "You're horrible. Griffin's gonna be mad."

She shrugs, and we walk through her house out onto her back patio. The pool they installed last year is still closed, but her comfy outdoor furniture is nice to sit on and enjoy the perfect spring day.

She tucks her legs underneath her. "So what did he say?"

"He said he wants us back."

"What an asshole," she says.

I hesitated to come here because I knew how she'd be. Phoenix will never warm to Jamison.

"I told him there was no chance for us."

"Of course! Can you imagine? He's such an arrogant prick."

I run my hands over my belly. "He wants to know whose baby it is."

She snickers. "And what did you say? Did you tell him?"

"No."

Her snicker turns into a full-on laugh. "Good. It's none of his business."

Her animosity upsets me, but it shouldn't. She's being protective of Palmer and me. I'd be the same way if the roles were reversed. Not to mention I was all "crucify Jamison, burn him at the stake" until he showed back up. Now all I think of is Palmer and the fact that she deserves to have her dad in her life. I just have to figure out if Jamison is worthy of that title.

"Regardless, he's her dad and I have to see where this is gonna go."

She rolls her eyes and lets out an annoyed huff. "No, you don't actually. Do you really think if his career didn't blow up, he'd be here? Think about it. He has nothing else in his life right now. What happens when he finds his next dream or finds himself looking at the bottom of a bottle again? You two will be in his rearview mirror."

I stand in a huff. Damn, my back is killing me. I forgot the crappy things that come with being pregnant. "Can we please not go there at this point? I don't have a crystal ball and I can't forecast the future. Neither of us can." I rub my lower back as I waddle toward the pool.

"He's already softened you." She throws her arms up in front of her. "God, that's it. We're doing the switcharoo." She raises her finger and twirls it in a circle.

I stare at her. "We're a little old for that. Plus, I'm pretty sure he'd figure it out."

"I wouldn't be so sure. I could convince him otherwise."

"Not unless you were in your third trimester."

Her face falls at the realization.

"And anyway, we're not switching on him."

"Then grow a fucking backbone. He can't just show up now after you've picked up all the broken pieces he left behind and expect you to bow at his feet." She meets me at the pool's edge.

"Just stop. I know, okay? But Palmer is his daughter. She deserves to have a relationship with him."

"He deserves a shit bomb on his front porch. Or a punch to his junk. He doesn't deserve to have that sweet girl wrap her arms around him and call him daddy."

I blow out a breath. "Imagine Maverick not even knowing Maggie. Look what you did to make sure she stayed in his life."

Her features soften. Sometimes with Phoenix, she just can't see anyone else's side but her own. She nods, then sighs. "Just do me a favor and don't let him Rico Suave you, okay?" She places her hand on my shoulder.

I shake my head as if that's the most absurd thought ever. "Of course not."

"Hey, you two." Griffin walks in, a sweaty mess, with Palmer in his arms.

Her eyes light up when she sees me. *Mommy.*

"Thanks so much, Griffin," I say, taking Palmer from him.

Daddy. She points at Griffin.

I blow out a breath and give Phoenix a look.

"You may have a point," she says and laughs.

Griffin goes in to kiss her and Phoenix pushes him away because he's too sweaty, but he runs his cheek along hers and she giggles until he captures her.

"Gross," Maverick says. "Hey, Aunt Sedona." He sits on the lounger and starts playing on his phone.

Palmer squirms out of my hold, and crawls up next to him on the lounger to watch.

"You got back sooner than I thought," Phoenix says and smiles at me.

Griffin raises his eyebrows. "Because your plan backfired on you."

"What plan?" she asks innocently with wide eyes.

"Sedona, sit down." Grandma Dori comes out of the house with Ethel in tow. "You need to be resting. Keep that baby in as long as you can. Especially with all the stress of that good-for-nothing boy showing back up here."

Griffin laughs and bops Phoenix on the end of the nose with his index finger. "I'm going to take a shower." Then he disappears into the house.

Grandma Dori leads me over to the couch, physically putting my feet up on the table while I give Phoenix the death stare of all death stares. I'm not sure what will end up being more painful—this meeting with Grandma Dori and Ethel, or the one I had earlier with Jamison.

FOUR

Jamison

I arrive back at Glacier Point and take the elevator up to my floor, half expecting my stuff to be sitting in the hallway. To be honest, I was surprised it wasn't already waiting with Mac the bellhop.

But once I turn the corner to my room, I'm faced with something I wasn't expecting—Kingston leaning against my door with his arms crossed.

"King," I say with a nod.

He nods in return and waits for me to use my keycard to gain access into my room. "We need to talk."

Sliding in front of me, he enters my room, looking around as if he expects to find someone here. He sits in one of the two chairs by the small table next to the window that looks out at Lake Starlight. I sit at the end of the bed.

Kingston's never been overly protective of his sisters, so I'm surprised he's the Bailey here. I feared the wrath of Phoenix more than Kingston, but he clearly has a connection with my daughter. One I'm already jealous of.

"Go ahead and say what you need to." I untie my shoes and place them under the luggage holder, where my small suitcase holds only a week's worth of clothes.

"I loved you like my brother and wanted you to be part of this family, but you abandoned her and that puts us on different terms now. Do you have any idea what she's had to deal with? What it was like for her?"

I run my hand through my hair. "I don't, no. And I know this is hard to understand right now, but the way I was when Sedona was pregnant... I wasn't good for either of them. It took a long time for me to realize that Sedona leaving me was the best thing that could have happened."

A hollow laugh escapes him. "Why? Because it got you clean? Still an egotistical asshole, huh?"

I lock my gaze with his. "No. Because I could've harmed Palmer." Her name still doesn't roll off my tongue like it should. "You have no idea how bad it was because I know Sedona hid my problem from you guys, but I was fucked up, man. She did what she should have."

He leans back in his chair. "How did it get so out of control?"

I bury my head in my hands, my toes sinking into the soft carpet that comes with a top-notch resort like Glacier Point. "I don't know. I was depressed. After the first injury to my ankle, they said take it easy and I'd be back up and ready in no time. But I probably shouldn't have played on it that soon. I rushed it. Told my coach I was ready when I probably wasn't, but fuck, playing soccer was my everything."

"My sister could have been your everything." He sneers.

I can't fault him. He's right. But pathetically, it wasn't that way. "True, but soccer was my first love." He opens his mouth, but I put my hand up to stop him. "I'm just being straight. That was then. It's been a long road to recovery to get my priorities in order. And they are now. Sedona and Palmer are all I want. Sedona isn't available and I'm not going to fuck up her life any more than I already have, but Palmer is still my daughter."

"Did Sedona tell you that?" He props his ankle on his knee while a smirk he can't win the fight against rests on his lips.

"Pretty much. Not to mention she's pregnant with some other guy's baby. She told me this morning anything between us is off the table." My heart still physically hurts when I think that I destroyed my future so thoroughly.

"True."

I peek up. "Who's the guy? I mean, do I know him? Is he from high school?"

I shouldn't ask Kingston, but I'm dying to know. How serious is this? Does the guy have a relationship with Palmer? She's clearly attached to Kingston. Was the guy at the shower yesterday? I have so many questions. I respected Sedona when she told me it was none of my business. She owes me nothing and I can't force myself into her heart no matter how bad it hurts that I lost my chance.

"If Sedona doesn't want to say, I won't tell you." He stands.

I forgot how intimidating the Bailey men are. They all stand over six feet with broad shoulders and scowls that have you second-guessing anything you said and did in the last twenty-four hours. And that's on a good day. Kingston's scowl right now is the worst I've seen.

I stand and match his height.

He huffs as though he's realized I'm no longer just his little sister's boyfriend. "It goes without saying, you hurt either of them and your ankle will be the last of your worries."

He doesn't crack his knuckles, but I feel as if he wants to.

"I just want to get to know my daughter."

"Speaking of, how do you know how to sign?"

"My uncle was deaf. He died when I was in high school, but..."

He nods. "Good thing for you she got Sedona's brain. She's smart as a whip and already ahead of kids her age. Then again, Sedona's been signing to her since she was an infant."

I nod, not acknowledging his insult. If Sedona passed her smarts down to Palmer, then I'm a happy father.

I have so many questions I want to ask Kingston about my daughter, but more than that, I want to find out for myself. My entire body itches to spend time with Palmer. To have her smile at me, or to have me be the one to protect her.

I put out my hand. "Thanks for doing what I should have."

He stares at my hand and laughs. "Your thanks can be to do right by them." He stuffs his hands into his pockets and heads to the door. "Just remember if I have to come find you again, it'll be to kick your ass." He opens the door and laughs uncontrollably. "Hey, G'Ma D. Your presence isn't necessary. I've already put the fear of death in him."

Dori slaps her grandson in the stomach. "Please, you don't scare a fly."

"I take offense to that." Kingston turns, following her with his gaze as she walks past me and occupies the chair he just got up from.

He shakes his head and turns to leave again, but another

senior citizen comes in holding a six-pack of cans. She thrusts them into Kingston's stomach.

"From my grandsons' brewery," she says.

Kingston shuffles to grab a hold of them before they fall to the floor. He picks them up and inspects them. "Your grandsons own Truth or Dare Brewery?"

Why does that name sound so familiar?

She nods. "Yep, in Sunrise Bay."

Bingo. I passed a restaurant with the logo that's on the beer can.

"How did I not know this, Ethel?" Kingston takes one can, beelines to his grandma, and sets the rest down between them. Then he sits on the bed and cracks it open.

"I have no idea. Maybe because you just recently started hanging around Lake Starlight again?"

Kingston gulps down a sip. "Damn, Ethel, this is awesome."

"She's like their pimp. They asked her to share it with people in Lake Starlight to try to increase their business." Dori eyes me. "Enough of that now. I need to talk to Jamison."

She exchanges a look with Kingston, and he stands, takes the rest of the beer from the table, and eyes me. "Come on, Ethel, let's go pimp your grandson to Wyatt. Maybe he'll put their beer in the restaurant." He swings his arm around the old lady who has hair that's more silver than gray.

They leave, and Dori pats the table. "Come sit, Jamison. We need to have a conversation about how this is gonna go."

"How what's gonna go?" I stand and sit across from her.

"You returning to Lake Starlight. Your relationship with Sedona and my great-granddaughter."

I open my mouth, but she raises her hand. For a

moment, I contemplate whether the Bailey men learned their intimidation tactics from Dori.

"I'll do the talking and you do the listening."

I nod.

"I'm all for you returning, and I hope you've got your life squared away. Unlike others in my family, I'm glad you're here. Sedona and Palmer need you in their lives."

I scrunch my eyebrows, not understanding why Sedona would need me. She's always been pretty independent. But I know better than to interrupt Dori, so I keep quiet.

"Palmer needs a dad. Hell, she's already tried to call Kingston daddy."

There's that sword slicing my heart as if it's made of paper again.

"Then Griffin earlier today. What is she supposed to think? Maverick has a dad. Easton has a dad. Lance and Brinley have dads. They all have dads and she wants to know where her dad is." Her voice grows more agitated.

"I—"

"Nope. If you can't be quiet, how can I assume you'll listen to my next set of instructions?" She raises one gray eyebrow, and I sink down in my chair. "Now, you're her daddy, but Sedona isn't going to tell her that right away. She'd be a fool to put that much trust in you at this point. Then again, you weaken Sedona. Always have." She shakes her head.

My shoulders sag. I never want to weaken her. Ever.

"She holds a soft spot for you no matter what. So ears open." She waits until I straighten in my seat. "This is going to take a lot of groveling and time to prove that you've changed. I hope you're ready. I'm on your side in regard to Palmer, but don't do anything stupid to make me change my mind. I've talked with Wyatt and Brooklyn and you're allowed to stay here as long as you'd like. They aren't going to kick you out."

"How did you—"

"I know everything that happens in this town. You've been away too long if you forgot that." She taps her temple then stands. "I better go save Ethel before she drinks too much again." Straightening her purse on her arm, she stares at me. "I always liked you, Jamison, until I hated you. I'm trusting you to stand up and do the right thing here. I hope we don't ever have to have another conversation like this, but that's solely up to you." She walks to the door and I stand. "Use those dimples and that charm, my boy. Palmer's easy—she wants you in her life. Sedona will be the real challenge."

"But I thought Sedona is with someone?" I call right before she opens the door.

She holds steady and doesn't turn around. "Did she tell you she's with someone?"

"Not exactly, but I mean, she's pregnant with someone's baby."

Her bluish-gray head nods. "Well, you'll find out soon enough."

"What does—"

The door shuts with a click. What the hell is going on?

FIVE

Sedona

Being pregnant for the second time is so much easier than the first. Then again, I don't have the heavy heart I had when I was pregnant with Palmer. Being asked about the father doesn't bring me that feeling of shame. If anything, this time around, people in town beam at the father and look at me as if I'm an angel.

One thing that hasn't changed is my nerves whenever I'm at the doctor's office for an appointment. But overall, I'm more relaxed and at peace this time around. I see how my mom was able to have so many kids.

The exam room is the same as always—the table situated by the window, two visitor chairs by the desk with the computer on it, and a doctor's stool on wheels tucked underneath the desk. The posters depicting the inside of a pregnant woman at various stages of her pregnancy make me look at my swollen belly with amazement every visit.

Still, there's a buzzing inside me. A feeling of being off-kilter that I can't shake. Jamison being back in my life at the same point as I was pregnant with Palmer when I left him has warped me back to that time in my life. The hurt and confusion, that feeling that I wasn't enough, have replanted and sprouted up inside me. But I refuse to allow my fear to be my demise.

A short knock and Dr. Estes pokes her head in. "Ready for me?"

I nod and she opens the door fully, leaving it slightly ajar.

"I just saw Daddy rush into the waiting room." She smiles and sits on her stool.

I stiffen at the news that he's here, and a new form of tension wraps around me. He's going to see right through me, and he's going to ask about Jamison. And I'm already about a minute from breakdown just from thinking about him.

"How are you feeling?" she asks.

But my attention is on the door. He must've rushed over on his lunch. Last we discussed, he couldn't make today's visit. "I'm good."

She types a few things on the computer. "Any contractions?"

"Nope."

"Since your first delivery went smoothly, I don't anticipate anything different with this one."

A soft knock lands on the door even though it's ajar.

Dr. Estes smiles at me like *get a load of this guy*. "You can come in."

Easton walks in first with a Dum Dum sucker in his mouth. I see now what took them so long to get from the reception area to the exam room. My nephew likes to stop and check out everything, and he always has a million questions. Austin peers in as though he's afraid I'm in the stirrups already.

"I called in a sub at the last minute. I didn't want to miss your appointment," Austin says.

I give him a warm smile.

"Hey, you." Dr. Estes raises her hand in a high five for Easton, and he slaps hers.

His auburn hair from Holly has already turned darker like Austin's, but his cute freckles are all Holly shining through.

"I heard you're going to be a big brother," Dr. Estes says.

"Yup," Easton says and turns to me. "Aunt Sedona, can I touch your belly?"

Easton's been obsessed with my stomach, always talking to it and touching it. Telling the baby what he's going to do for it and what his parents are doing to prepare for her. He's going to be the best big brother.

"Let the doctor check me out first," I say.

He crawls up on the waiting chair. The chairs that were usually empty when I was pregnant with Palmer.

"And Mommy? Where's she?" Dr. Estes asks Austin.

"Holly's stuck at work." He touches my shoulder. "You doing okay?"

I suck back my emotions. This is such a happy time for my brother and Holly, and I'm not going to ruin it with my own shit. I offered to carry their baby after Holly suffered two miscarriages. The fertility treatments had already cost them so much money and I couldn't bear to see them go through any more disappointment. After Austin stepped in to raise me when our parents died, carrying his baby is the least I can do.

"I'm great." I smile, hoping he's so preoccupied with his upcoming responsibilities of having two children that he won't notice my anxiety twisting its way through my body, wringing me tight.

His lips tip down, and I sigh. Yeah, guess not. Austin's practically my father. Since I was eight, he's the one who raised me and saw me through my pre-adolescent and teenage years. He was there, warning me when I first met Jamison, making sure my door was open. Being a teacher at our high school, he saw us and worried we were growing too close for our age and stage of life.

Dr. Estes does my exam. I'm measuring thirty-seven weeks now. Easton kisses my belly and his eyes light up when he hears the heartbeat, placing his ear exactly where Dr. Estes had the instrument.

On the way out, Easton puts one of his hands in mine and the other in Austin's, another Dum Dum stick sticking out of his mouth.

"You want to talk?" Austin asks me, stopping by my car.

I'm parked by an open grassy area and Easton walks along the curb as if it's a tightrope.

"No. I'm fine. He's meeting us at the park tomorrow."

Austin nods. "Did you tell him about..." His gaze dips to my large belly.

"No. I know I should. It's childish and mean to allow him to think—"

"Hell no. That guy deserves to think you've moved on."

Moved on? For the last eighteen months, I've been at a standstill. I've carried on with my life, but I'm not really living it.

"Can I ask you a question?"

He eyes Easton and shifts his attention back to me. "Anytime."

"You and Holly, do you guys fight? I mean, is everything perfect?"

His lips tick up and a belly laugh erupts out of him. "Um… no. Why on Earth would you think that?"

I shrug. "You guys seem happy."

His laugh abruptly stops. "We are happy, but we're not perfect. All couples fight."

Easton starts repeating his ABCs, skipping over L through P. Austin stops Easton from going from K to Q and has him repeat after him. Always the teacher.

"I just wondered. I mean, Mom and Dad were always so happy."

His shoulders sink and he inhales a deep breath. "Being the oldest sucks at times. I've had to pop your happy bubble so many times over the years that I feel like the fucking Grinch stealing your youth. Marriage is hard work, Sedona. I know you, Phoenix, and Kingston never saw Mom and Dad fight, and this town paints their love story like a bestselling romance novel. Truth is, they fought, they made up. I think they were happy. They smiled and laughed a lot. Kept having kids." He chuckles. "But their love wasn't as perfect as this town wishes it were. You guys just don't remember. Nothing is ever perfect. You take the good with the bad."

"I know."

He lowers to look into my eyes. "Do you? Listen to me, knowing Jamison from before he started drinking, I think he's a good guy who veered onto the wrong path." I open my mouth, but he holds up his hand. "Let me finish. I'm not saying take him back. Not even close to that. Everything has come easy to you two until this. Maybe I have a soft spot because he lost the career he thought he was destined for, and I understand what that does to someone. Not that I'd change anything in my life, but for years after I returned, I would've done everything to get back to where I was before our parents died. Then Holly arrived in Lake Starlight and what I envisioned for my future changed. That doesn't happen for everyone. I think some people get stuck."

"That's the thing though. I was already in his life. I was second to soccer then, and I dealt with it. Now that he can't have his first love, it's like I'm sloppy seconds." It's the first time I've said that to anyone, although I always felt second best to his soccer career.

He stuffs his hands in his pockets and stares at the blue sky. "The guy grew up with a love for soccer. I doubt he ever thought of you as second, but that doesn't negate your feelings either. All you can really do now is allow him to get to know Palmer. She deserves to have a dad if he wants to be a part of her life. No one said you have to allow him back into your heart."

"So just allow him to get close enough to her to risk hurting her?"

"Easton, careful." He looks from his son back to me and places both hands on my shoulders. "I'm going to tear off the Band-Aid, okay?" His eyes bore into mine and I nod, biting my lip. "You need to take yourself out of the equation. You need to focus solely on his relationship with Palmer. If the two of you try to get back together, that just complicates things and has the capacity to ruin Palmer's relationship with her father—or make it more difficult at the very least. I can't speak for raising a kid without being partners with his mother, but I have to think that the better you two work together, the better off Palmer is. So right now, it's probably best to concentrate on Jamison and Palmer's relationship, not yours and Jamison's."

I swallow past the lump in my throat.

Austin calls Easton back over when he strays a little too far and tells him they're going to go.

Easton walks under his dad's arms and hugs and kisses my belly. "Bye-bye, sista. Bye, Aunt Sedona."

I nod at Austin, letting him know I understand the advice he's given, and crouch to Easton's level to give him a big hug. I'm rewarded with a kiss on the cheek. Children are so sweet and innocent before life takes the floor out from beneath their feet.

"Hang in there. After you get that one out, your hormones won't be interfering." Austin nods toward my stomach and shoots me his gentle smile that displays how grateful he is I sacrificed my body for nine months to grow his daughter.

I'd do it as many times as he needs me to. God knows he put his life on hold for me.

"Thanks, Austin."

"Give Palmer a hug and a kiss from us." He snatches Easton up before he runs into the parking lot.

"I will. Love you." I blow a kiss and Easton giggles, blowing one back.

Once I'm alone in my car, I pull out of the doctor's office parking lot. My mind can't stop thinking about the first time I met Jamison and how perfect our destiny seemed then.

SIX

Sedona

Seventeen years old

Phoenix slams her locker. "The nerve of him. Telling me to 'buckle down on my studies.'" My twin sister imitates our oldest brother, Austin, with a scowl.

Whereas I've always felt sad that Austin had to return home after college to raise us, Phoenix challenges him at every turn. What should've been the fun-filled years of his twenties, playing pro baseball and enjoying life, have been spent raising my siblings and me after our parents died. He's only trying to get Phoenix to take her future seriously. He's always stuck between the older brother and father role.

"Don't just stand there and say nothing," she says, leaning against her locker.

I dig into mine, switching my biology book for my calculus one. "I don't disagree with him. I get that you're all in for the theater group doing *Grease* this year, but if you want to go to college, they want the grades too."

She shrugs, pulls out a piece of gum and pops it into her mouth, nodding to people passing through the hallways. "Maybe I don't want to go to college. Kingston didn't."

I roll my eyes, remembering the fights between him and Austin. Even now that he's graduated from the fire academy, Austin still thinks Kingston's life should've taken a different path.

"If they'd give me my money, there wouldn't be a problem."

"You know that money is only for college."

We walk down the hall. She's got English while I'm in calculus. "Again, I bring up Kingston. I swear he's Austin's favorite."

"I don't think he has a favorite," I say.

"Well, I think I'm the one he hates the most. See you." She turns left into her classroom as I turn right.

I blow out a breath and decide to concentrate on what I can control—getting out of Lake Starlight and following my mom's footsteps of traveling the world and writing about it. She never explained it, or maybe I was too young to understand, but I've always wondered why a woman who chose to be a travel writer decided to have nine kids and raise them in a small town. I guess love is powerful when it's right. Last year when I was digging through the basement, looking for my ice skates, I found her diary from when she was sixteen. She had so many hopes and dreams until she fell in love with my dad.

Walking to my desk, I nod a hello to my classmates, who I've known forever. It's rare for anyone new to move to Lake Starlight. Which means I'll be waiting until college to meet anyone special. Don't get me wrong, some of the boys here are cute. They just don't do it for me. I'll have to go to prom with someone, but as I scan the classroom, no one piques my interest.

Calculus is boring and hard, and I hate it. Why can't I be in English with Phoenix?

Fifty minutes later, the bell rings and a pit of excitement fills my belly. It's my lunch period, but since I work on the high school newspaper as editor-in-chief, I can go to the deserted classroom we morphed into our office.

Once I'm there, I take a bite of my turkey sandwich and boot up the computer. Grabbing the file folder in my inbox from Kasey, our sports reporter, I open it to find her resignation. Only she would actually write a resignation letter for a school newspaper. She says she doesn't have the time to commit to the paper since she now has a part-time job at Lard Have Mercy. Great.

The information for the article I assigned her last week is still sitting there with nothing added, no research done.

She was supposed to highlight the new foreign exchange student who's attending Lake Starlight High this year. Now that I think of it, it's weird that I haven't seen a new face yet. We must run on opposite schedules.

Miles breezes through the door with his tray in his hands.

"Nancy's still mesmerized by those dimples of yours, I see." Miles is the only person Nancy, the lunch lady, allows to leave the cafeteria with a tray.

"Actually, I think I lost her. She's drooling over the new kid from Scotland's accent."

"The new foreign exchange student?"

He slides up on the desk, picking up his piece of greasy pizza. "Yeah, in fact, he's sitting with a table full of girls right now." Then he pretends to talk in a Scottish accent.

"Look at me, I'm mister cool guy from a different country. Yeah, I play *football*."

"That was a horrible accent," I say.

He takes another bite of his pizza. "They're treating him like a god in there," he mumbles with food in his mouth.

"Jealousy doesn't look good on you."

He shrugs, finishing his pizza, and pops open the can of soda he must've gotten from the vending machine.

"I have to interview him. Kasey quit."

He hops down from the table. "Good luck. The guy is a narcissist."

"Slight exaggeration?"

He boots up his own computer. "Maybe. You know me, I hate competition, and that fucker is going to get my spot on first string."

So that's where all the animosity is coming from. "Hey, do you have soccer practice today?"

He nods, sipping his soda.

"Cool, I'll try to grab him to set up an interview time then."

"Ha! Our practices are pretty popular now. You'll probably have to make an appointment."

Whatever. Miles is used to being the good-looking guy in our class. He's the managing editor for the newspaper, class president, and captain of the soccer team. All-around great guy who treats everyone with respect. Usually it's him with the girls swarming his locker, so I'm sure this is just jealousy.

Just like I'm sure this new guy can't be that special. The girls in our school are just tired of looking at the same old boys, that's all.

SO, I was wrong.

Miles was right. Thank God I didn't bet him.

The new foreign exchange student, Jamison Ferguson, is hot. Like HAWT hot. He runs up and down the field, masterfully handling the ball with his feet. Miles wears a red mesh shirt to signify he's on a different team. Jamison stops the ball with his foot, pivots, and leaves Miles stretched out on the field as he easily moves around Miles and shoots the ball into the goal. Jamison's arms fly up and he runs to his teammates for hugs and congratulations.

Poor Miles picks at the grass and throws it back down, getting to his feet.

The coach calls practice and I walk down the bleachers, along with a bunch of other girls—Jamison's new fan club. They wave and smile and giggle as he raises his shirt to wipe his face, showing off a set of abs that you could literally wash clothes on. My core tingles with excitement.

Jamison's gaze scatters across his new fans until they land on me. He scowls. Meanwhile, my stomach is fluttering, my entire body tingling with want.

He puts his focus back on the other girls. Guess I'm alone in that feeling then.

He's swarmed, all the girls asking about where he learned to play and why he chose to come to Alaska. All the same questions I have written down to ask him.

"I told you," Miles says, swinging his sweaty arm over my shoulders.

"I need an in. This is insane."

"Wait until after he showers. Coach tells them all to go home. I'll introduce you two." He winks before heading toward the locker room.

Jamison walks away, waving to the girls, but he glances at me and stops before jogging over. My throat closes up the closer he comes. His blue eyes twinkle, even without any light on them. His dark hair drips with sweat, but his body is deliciously packaged with lean muscle.

Once he stands in front of me, he towers over me. "Why are you here? Still trying to figure out why I'm not wearing a kilt?"

"What?" I blink in surprise at the animosity tone in his voice. "Kilt?"

"Yeah, you know. You assuming all Scots are red-haired, pasty, and wear a kilt with nothing underneath?"

I shake my head. "I have no idea what you're talking about."

His eyes narrow and he steps back. "Sure, you don't."

Before I can say anything, he jogs away and disappears into the building. That's when it dawns on me and I pull out my phone. Phoenix answers on the first ring.

"Did you talk to the new foreign exchange student?" I ask.

"Ugh, isn't he annoying? That accent of his is clearly exaggerated. And I asked him where his kilt was and whether he wears anything under it, and he got all offended. It can't be the first time someone's asked."

I shake my head. "Well, he just confused me for you."

"You should feel lucky. The guy is a class-A asshole who thinks he's God's gift to women."

"I'll see you at home." I hang up and round the front of the school to the parking lot.

Austin's ridiculous Jeep with that damn snorkel on it is parked in the front row. Maybe Miles can give me a ride so I don't have to be seen in that thing again today.

Sitting at the picnic table, I go over my questions. Some

of the parents of the soccer players pull up along the curb to pick them up, and I'm thinking the interview isn't going to happen today.

The school doors open, and a group of guys walk out. Miles points me out to Jamison. He's not scowling anymore, so that's good.

"Jamison, this is *Sedona* Bailey," Miles says, which means he's already explained the twin thing.

Jamison puts out his hand. His hair is now damp from the shower and his body smells like pure man. A pair of low-slung sweatpants rest on his hips, and he wears a sweatshirt with Aberdeen Football Club stamped on it. "I'm sorry I acted like an arse."

Now that he's not so angry, I take better notice of his accent. Oh my God, it's divine.

I nod, my voice lost somewhere deep down in my throat. "It's okay. It happens."

There's a hint of calluses on his palm, but electricity flies up my arm at his touch.

He clears his throat. "So, Miles said you wanted to interview me for the newspaper?"

I nod.

Miles shakes his head at me because I'm blabbering like one of his groupies.

I clear my throat. "Whenever you're available."

"How about Friday night? We could meet somewhere?" Jamison offers.

I almost melt to the ground. "Yeah, sure."

Miles rolls his eyes.

"Cool." Jamison runs his hand through his hair.

I wonder what that feels like. I clench my hand harder on my notepad.

"Six o'clock at that diner place in town?" He turns to Miles and adds, "I love their pies."

Miles nods and huffs.

"I'll be there," I say.

"Cool." Jamison steps away. Thank goodness because I might just faint. He stops short. "Sorry again about earlier, lass."

Omg, he called me lass!

I shake my head. "No problem. I'm fully aware of how Phoenix can be."

"Great meeting you, Sedona." His gaze falls down my body once before he leaves, climbing into his host parent's car.

"Another one bites the dust," Miles says, tugging on my arm. "I'll drive you home. But please put your tongue back in your mouth. I don't want drool all over my seats."

I climb into Miles's truck and all I can think about is Jamison. Is this how my mom felt when she met my dad? I'll bet it is.

SEVEN

Sedona

Palmer's favorite thing to do at the park is play in the sandbox. As I sit on the bench watching her, my anxiety increases my heart rate tenfold. Any second, her father is going to show up. Palmer's always curious about anyone new, and I know she's going to ask questions.

She scoops sand into the fish mold and dumps it over, all of the loose sand spilling out before the mold presses into the sand. Then she picks up the fish and looks at it quizzically, and her shoulders slump.

She's so amazing. So sweet and open to anyone she meets. It's that aspect of her little personality that kept me up late last night. She'll open her arms wide for Jamison. How will he react?

"Hey," he announces himself before coming into my peripheral vision.

I inhale and close my eyes for a second. I open them, Palmer's already ditched the sandbox to walk over to us.

Jamison rounds the bench. He's dressed in jeans and a

sweatshirt, and the fresh scent of his soap wafts by me before he sits next to me.

"Hey," I say.

Palmer stands in front of him and stares.

Jamison glances at me and back at her. *Hello, how are you?*

Why am I irritated that he can sign? I should be thrilled that I'm finally able to narrow down why Palmer was born deaf. The fact he can so easily communicate with her is a plus, not a minus, but I hate it just the same.

Palmer waves to him and looks at me. *Who?*

Jamison remains still, allowing me the right to decide how I want to introduce him.

"I'm sorry. I'm just not ready yet." I don't look at him when I speak or sign. *Friend.*

Palmer smiles and turns all her attention to Jamison. Grabbing his hand, she leads him over to the sandbox, where he sits on the edge. Palmer picks up the fish mold and holds it out for him, grunting for him to take it. He smiles and accepts it, then he presses the sand into the fish mold, completing the task she tried to do minutes earlier. Palmer smiles wide, clapping with her mouth wide open in surprise. Jamison beams with happiness as he stares at her, and my stomach twists in knots.

I can't get over how healthy he looks. How carefree he appears compared to when I left him and the weight of the world was on his shoulders.

I'm not sure how long I sit there, lost in my thoughts.

"Sedona?" Jamison's hand on my shoulder pulls me back from reliving the nightmare our love affair turned into.

"I'm sorry, what?" I search for Palmer, but she's in the sandbox.

"Did you want to grab lunch?"

"Oh sure," I say before I think better of it. Palmer has a routine I rarely stray from. "Actually, we can't. It's her nap time."

Palmer walks over. *Hungry*. Then she puts her hand in Jamison's. Jamison raises his eyebrows at me, and my shoulders fall.

I sign back *quick* and Palmer smiles at Jamison. There goes that gut twist again. It's like a wet towel that keeps getting wrung out, tighter and tighter.

"Let's go then," I say, a little annoyed.

I pack up her sand toys, and we leave the park with Palmer's hand in both of ours as if we're a happy little family. I can barely stomach it.

We reach Lard Have Mercy and are seated in a booth overlooking the gazebo. We place our orders with the waitress and make awkward chitchat about mundane topics.

"She's beautiful," Jamison says, staring at Palmer who's now draped over my chest, asleep.

Karen comes over, sets our orders down in front of us, and runs her hand down Palmer's back. Then she kisses her hand and places it on my belly. "I can't wait to spoil this one."

I smile. Karen is Austin's wife's mom, but she's also married to my uncle now, so I guess she's more like my stepaunt. Although I still think of her as Holly's mom.

"Soon, I think," I say.

Jamison's jaw twitches. He hasn't asked me once today whose baby it is. Good. Let him suffer.

"Karen, you remember Jamison?"

Karen glances over her shoulder and nods. "Hello."

It's the coldest hello I've ever heard from her lips.

Jamison nods. "Hi. How are you? Enjoying your grandson?"

She eyes me for a moment, not granting him her full attention. "Anything else, sweetie?"

"No. I'm fine." I smile widely and look at my turkey club. Between my stomach and Palmer, none of it will make it into my mouth.

As though Jamison has been a part of our life forever, he quickly realizes my dilemma. Rising from his seat, he comes to the side of the booth where I'm sitting, hands held out. "May I?"

I leave him standing there with his arms extended. Do I really want to grant him the gift of holding our sleeping child? It's one of my favorite moments with my daughter. I can just stare at her and smile at the peaceful look on her face, hoping her life is easier than mine—except for those fleeting years we were together in New York when things were good.

The perfect job. The perfect condo. The perfect boyfriend.

My stomach growls and I know I need to eat. This baby needs to remain healthy.

I hand her over, and he takes Palmer to his side of the booth and positions her in his arms like an actual baby, her head tucked into his elbow.

"Your arm will go numb like that." With much effort, I slide out of the booth and pick her up. I place her chest on his, draping her arms over his shoulders so her face is in the crook of his neck. It's her favorite position. Palmer sighs. "There you go."

"Thanks." He holds her with both hands, one across her butt and the other cradling her head.

"You can still eat if you'd like. She sleeps like a rock."

"Just like me, huh?"

We fall silent for a moment. Like me, he's likely remembering the joke between us about how he could sleep through a family of elephants pounding through our apartment.

"Yeah," I say and pick up my turkey sandwich.

He eyes me. "I hate this, Sedona. This awkwardness that's never been there between us before."

I know what he means. Since the first time I interviewed him in high school, we just clicked. And although years passed while I was at NYU and he was playing in the Scottish Premiership, when he showed up on my doorstep in New York, nothing had changed.

"This isn't some great reunion, Jamie."

He smiles over his burger.

I scowl. "What?"

"It's the first time you called me Jamie."

Rolling my eyes, I say, "Some habits are hard to break."

"Maybe," he murmurs.

He puts down his burger and wipes his hand with a napkin, then he runs his hand down Palmer's back like a concerned father. One who's been present in her life.

Shit, anger is pulsing through my veins again. I need to stop this, for Palmer's sake.

My shoulders fall and my nose tickles. Tears are coming and I'm not going to be able to stop them. I glance around to see how busy the diner is, praying no one snaps a picture for Buzz Wheel right now. The last thing I need is a headline detailing how my entire life is falling apart.

"Do you honestly think you're staying here?" A tear slips out and I press my palm to my cheek, smearing it away.

"In Lake Starlight or in your life?" he asks.

"I guess I thought they were one and the same."

He leans back in the booth, balling up his napkin and throwing it on the plate. "I want the two of you back more than anything. But if I'm honest, there's no job for me here. I've applied for some assistant coaching positions back home, not that I'm confident any of them will amount to anything."

"Where?"

"Manchester U, Arsenal, Celtic," he says, his gaze falling to Palmer, his hand gripping her tighter. "I'd likely have to start in their youth divisions and work my way up."

I slide out of the booth, take her out of his arms, and place her in the stroller.

"Wait, that doesn't change anything," he says.

"It doesn't change anything?" I yell and glance around before lowering my voice. "It changes everything," I whisper-shout. "This is Palmer's home. Here in Alaska, around people who care about us. Is that why you're back? Are you going to try to take her halfway across the world away from me?"

Karen comes over. "Sweetie, calm down." She helps me secure a now-crying Palmer in her stroller. She's reaching out to Jamison to return to his lap. Another waitress hands Karen a cookie and she passes it to my daughter. "There you go, sweetheart. Eat the cookie."

It mollifies Palmer enough that she stops crying.

"I'm not trying to take her anywhere. She's my daughter and I want a relationship with her." He slides out of the booth. "I'm trying to do this the right way."

I step up to him, silently cursing that I can't tower over him. "I'm not going to allow you to be all sweet and endearing like you give a shit about us. I thought you were here to be present in her life. What's the master plan? Worm your way into our lives and then convince me to move to Europe so you can live out some fantasy of being back on the celebrity circuit again? Then in a few years, I'm tucking my tail between my legs and coming back home to pitying looks. I have a life." I rub my belly. "In case you haven't noticed."

"I have noticed, and believe me, it kills me. Do you have any idea what seeing you pregnant with someone else's baby is doing to me?" he shouts back.

"Why should I care? You didn't even give a shit when I was carrying *your* baby!"

"Okay, you two." Karen rubs my back.

My gaze falls to Palmer, whose lower lip is trembling as cookie crumbs fall out of her mouth.

"I can't do this. I just can't." I grab the stroller, tears cascading down my face, wishing I could disappear. Damn hormones.

"Sedona," Jamison calls.

"You gotta give her time," Karen says. "This is the worst moment you could've picked to walk back into her life."

I circle around to push the diner door open with my back when a gripping pain hits my stomach. Liquid drips down my thighs. Not now. Not now. This cannot be happening.

"Karen," I say.

She turns from telling Jamison off and her face pales. Another waitress takes Palmer while Karen leads me to a booth.

"I'm fine. When my water broke with Palmer, I didn't deliver her for hours. Have Austin or Holly pick me up." I sit down, imposing on a nice older gentleman eating his tuna on rye. "Sorry about this."

"It's okay. My wife was pregnant six times and I feel like I should warn you. The first baby, she was in labor for thirty-six hours. The sixth baby was delivered in my truck on the side of the road." He eyes me.

I look down, half expecting the baby's head to be poking out.

"I'm driving you to the hospital." Jamison's hand lands on my arm and he pulls me to my feet.

"Um... no." I look past him at Karen, who has her cell phone to her ear. I hope Austin or Holly pick up.

"This is ridiculous. You'd rather wait for your older brother to show up than allow me to take you to the hospital? At least call the dad." He eyes me as I grip my stomach for a contraction I didn't think would come on so soon.

Maybe the man at my right is correct and this baby is coming sooner than I thought.

Palmer stops crying due to all the commotion, but she's looking around, trying to understand what's going on.

I wave my hand to get her attention. *I'm good. Baby.*

She signs back. *Hurt?*

I shake my head. I don't want her to worry about me. Realizing that someone will need to come get her, I pick up my cell phone and text Liam, hoping he's at the tattoo shop right now. He can at least get Palmer to one of my sisters.

Karen frantically hangs up and dials another number, staring at me with wide eyes.

Jamison is pacing, asking me if the person I'm calling is the father.

Thankfully, a couple minutes later, Liam opens the diner door and stops short, assessing the situation.

"You okay?" he asks me, and I nod.

I motion Palmer over to me. *You go with Liam. Play with Brinley. Mommy is having the baby.* I rub my belly.

Palmer presses her lips to my belly, but another contraction comes, and I hunch forward and blow out a breath.

Love you.

She signs back. *Love you.*

We hug, and Liam squeezes my shoulder before taking her with him out the door.

"Savannah will meet you at the hospital," Liam says and walks out with Palmer in one arm and pushing the stroller in front of him.

"This is ridiculous. I could've had her at the hospital by now."

I stand, and Karen is finally talking to someone. "Tell them to meet me at the hospital."

"Why do you care so much about Austin and Holly?" Jamison asks.

I allow him to help me because at this point, I have no choice but to accept his strength.

This is a totally different feeling than I had with Palmer.

The tires of Austin's Jeep screeches to a stop along the curb.

Karen sighs. "Thank goodness he made it."

Jamison glances around. "Why is Austin so important right now? Where the hell is the dad?"

Karen laughs. "Austin *is* the dad."

The other waitresses laugh, as do most of the people at the nearby tables because it's not a secret here in Lake Starlight—except, of course, to my ex.

Jamison's face pales. "Your brother is the father of your baby?"

EIGHT

Jamison

What the hell? Someone needs to wake me up. This must all be a dream. Sedona's baby daddy is Austin?

Speaking of, Austin swings open the door, taking Sedona from me and leading her to the passenger side of the vehicle.

"I can walk," she says, swatting him away. She glances back at me, then at her brother. "Where's Holly?"

"She's going to meet us. She was at a meeting up in Anchorage."

I feel like an idiot standing here watching these two.

"I'm waiting for Nancy to come and cover, then I'll meet you there," Karen hollers out the door then disappears back inside.

"I think we have to bring Jamison on the off chance that the baby comes before we reach the hospital." Sedona buckles over in pain, but I don't react this time.

Austin opens up the back door for Sedona to slide in and turns to me. "Let's go, Jamison. I guess you do get to experience Sedona in labor. Who would have thought?" Austin leaves the door open as he rounds the front of the Jeep.

"What?" I'm still so confused. I know my feet should be moving, but it's as if they're stuck in crazy glue.

"Let's go!" Austin yells, hanging out of his Jeep.

I run to the back and get in beside Sedona. She's breathing heavily.

"Remember your classes," Austin says, peeling around the corner.

"Can someone please tell me what the hell is going on?" I ask.

Austin glances at Sedona through the rearview mirror and she looks at me. Her hands are on her stomach and she's breathing in and out—hard. Is this what it was like for her when she had Palmer? Damn it all to hell, I missed so much, lost in an empty bottle of self-pity otherwise known as Glenfiddich.

"You okay?" I put my hand over hers. She doesn't immediately pull away.

"Ahhhh!" She moans when Austin turns a corner and hits the gas. "Hurry, Austin!"

"I am." His phone rings in the center console, but he glances down and doesn't answer it.

"Are you really pregnant with your brother's baby?" I whisper.

She turns to me and nods, biting her lip. I blanch.

"She's coming. I know it," she says.

"Jamison's going to need to check." Austin's Jeep stops. "A row of ducks is crossing the road."

Sedona groans.

Someone honks their horn over and over before pressing on it for a long time.

"Okay, do you want to lie back?" I offer. I'm not really sure what I'm looking for down there, but I guess if a baby is coming out, it'll be obvious.

"No!" She swats my hands away. "You're not seeing me deliver a baby."

"What? Why not?"

"Because."

"I would've if I'd been here for Palmer," I say. "I would've watched her come out of you. Hell, I've gone down on you how many times in my life?"

"TMI, buddy," Austin says from the front seat. Once the ducks have crossed, he turns the wheel to go around the other vehicles on the road but stops short, rolling down his passenger window. "Grandma!"

Sedona and I look out the window to find Dori at another driver's window, lecturing them about honking their horn. "Imagine you were trying to get across a highway and people were honking their horns at you." Then she looks over and her eyes widen. She scurries over and opens the front passenger door. "Ethel, meet me at the hospital!"

I glance back, and sure enough, Ethel is driving Dori's Cadillac one car back. She gives her friend a thumbs-up, then Austin weaves by the ducks, dodging the oncoming traffic.

Dori peers in the back. "How are you, sweetie?"

Sedona's busy breathing, her legs clamped together.

"She won't let me check," I say, hoping Dori can persuade Sedona.

"Oh no. Switch spots." Dori unbuckles herself.

Austin's arm goes out like the mom safety bar across

Dori's chest. "I'm almost there. You hanging in there?" he asks Sedona.

"So this must be a shock to you, Jamison." Dori settles back down in her seat.

"I'm good, but the contractions are so close. Where did you say Holly is?" Sedona's head falls to the window.

"Yer okay with this?" I ask Dori.

"I think it's great," Dori says. "Sweet actually."

I nod a few times. I know I'm missing something. I finally snap, needing to know exactly what's going on. "Come on. Is Austin seriously the father?" I whisper to Sedona.

Her head falls from side to side and she grips her stomach again. "How much longer?"

"We're here!" Austin says.

The Jeep's tires squeal around the corner and he slams on his brakes in front of the emergency room entrance.

Dori steps out of the Jeep and I head out on my side, but Austin grabs Sedona before I can, helping her around the back. He tosses me the keys. "Park my Jeep."

I grab them in the air and Dori pats me on the back. "Austin has to be there for the birth."

I watch the three of them walk into the emergency room and all I can concentrate on is everything I missed. The last eighteen months weighs on my shoulders. I ruined it all. She's made a whole life for herself without me in it. I know they're messing with me about her child being Austin's baby, which means she wants to shut me out completely.

I round the front of Austin's Jeep and remember how many times I wanted to drive this thing back in high school. I honestly can't believe he still owns it. He's taken really good care of it. After I pull into the parking lot, I sit for a moment and decide I'll leave the keys at the nurses' station and take an Uber back to the hotel. I might be a part of Palmer's future, but I'm clearly not going to be a part of Sedona's.

I'm crossing the pedestrian walkway when a car whizzes by, parking in a nearby spot.

Holly's out of her car in a flash. "Hey, Jamison." She waves and goes in.

Why is she in such a hurry?

Then, as if someone made an announcement over the Lake Starlight PA system, all the Baileys arrive in a parade of cars. Phoenix is the first one out of her car, and she flips me off behind Maverick's back as they head into the hospital.

My footsteps slow, and by the time I'm inside, Kingston's already at the nurses' station. Stella's coming down another hallway in her white doctor coat.

Ethel pops up beside me without warning, putting her arm through mine. "Escort me to the waiting area."

It's the last thing I want to do, but I do as she asks. "Sure."

We walk into the waiting room and she sits down. Some daytime talk show is playing on the TV in the empty room.

"Can I leave Austin's keys with you?" I ask, holding them out. "I'm going to head out."

She stares at the keys in my hand before patting the chair next to her. "You need to sit down."

"I shouldn't be here."

"Damn right you shouldn't!" Brooklyn's voice fills the entire room.

"Let's calm down," Wyatt says.

"See?" I say to Ethel.

She pats the chair again. "I'm under strict orders to keep you here."

"By whom?" Brooklyn asks, taking off Lance's coat and letting him go check out the books and blocks.

"Who do you think? Your grandmother."

Brooklyn crosses her arms. "I have no idea why Grandma Dori keeps allowing him to linger around. He left Sedona high and dry."

Wyatt blows out a breath and takes off his suit jacket, heading to where the kids are playing with Lance.

One by one, each Bailey finds their way to the waiting room after finding out that they're not allowed into the delivery room. Stella comes in for a second to say hi. She tells Kingston to let her know what happens, but she has patients to get back to. She's now working in the medical offices attached to the hospital. Thank God for Buzz Wheel or I wouldn't know any of this. They kiss, and when she leaves, Kingston stalks over next to me, picks up a magazine, and hums "Beat It" by Michael Jackson.

I'm about to leave when Austin walks into the waiting room. His eyes find mine first out of everyone, and my gut plummets to the floor below. Something is wrong.

"She's having an emergency C-section," he says to the room. "The doctor says it's okay, but the baby is in distress."

Kingston stands. "Shouldn't you be with her?"

"Only one person can go in. Holly's going to stay with her." Austin flops down in a chair and buries his head in his hands.

As the family surrounds him, I stalk out of the room, unable to show my real emotions around a family who hates me. I'm almost through the sliding doors, needing some fresh air, when Dori grabs my sleeve and leads me into a small room. She flips the lock but thankfully turns on the lights. This is not the scenario I imagined when I pictured a woman pulling me into a hidden room.

"Listen to me. The whole ballgame just changed. If you want Sedona back, you better straighten up and fly right. This is your time to prove to this family how much you love her and can't live without her."

"I don't understand. Tell me, whose baby is it? Where is he? Why is Holly the one in there holding her hand?"

Her eyebrows scrunch together. "Seriously? You haven't figured it out? I thought you were an honor student in high school?"

"I am. I was. I've asked a zillion times and no one will answer me."

She taps her finger to my temple. "Come on, Jamison. Use that brain of yours. There's been no father mentioned and there's no one here you don't know. Austin drove her to the hospital and Holly is the one in the operating room with her. Figure it out."

I think it all over. Them saying Austin is the father. I thought it was a joke. I know Austin and Holly had a hard time conceiving Easton...

Something must show in my eye because Dori nods, confirming what I'm thinking is correct. "She's carrying Austin and Holly's baby?"

"Bingo. You should play Words with Friends, it keeps the mind sharp." She taps her temple and pulls her phone from her purse.

I lean against the wall, processing the information, my breathing labored from the thought of losing her. The one woman I've loved my entire adult life is going to have surgery, and because of my own jackass moves, I'm not the one in there with her. All the what-ifs stack up in my brain and topple over, but with that comes a realization.

"So there isn't another man standing in my way," I mumble.

"Nope, there's not." Dori types something on her phone, not noticing me about to pass out from the sheer fear of never holding Sedona again.

My back slides along the wall as I sink to the floor with my head in my hands.

"Jamison, she's going to be fine. She's a Bailey." Dori doesn't lean down to comfort me, and she shouldn't. I'm scum.

"What if something happens during surgery? I could lose her before I'm able to win her back." I glance up at her. "What have I done?"

Dori steps up, towering over me. Her shoulders fall and her eyes soften. I've only ever seen this side of her on Bailey Founder's Day.

"Get up," she says.

I shake my head.

"This is my last time asking. Get up," she says.

I manage to get myself onto my feet.

"Usually I wouldn't be so gracious to someone who hurt my grandchild so badly, but I've always had a soft spot for you. And I understand what you're going through. Everyone deserves a second chance, but." Her finger raises. "Only a second. I don't do that 'third times a charm' crap, you hear me?"

I nod, having no idea what she's about to say.

"So I'm going to help you have access to Sedona, but I'm not going to convince her to take you back. That's her decision. But if you ruin this opportunity and my granddaughter and great-granddaughter get hurt, Ethel's grandson is a hitman and he owes me a lot of favors."

I laugh.

She doesn't.

My laugh dies. "Got it. How are you going—"

She holds up her hand. "I'm Dori Bailey. Are you really going to doubt me? Just be prepared when I call you."

She walks away and opens the door of the small room. Savannah, Liam, Palmer and Brinley walk into the hospital when we get into the hallway. Palmer squirms to get out of Savannah's arms, but Savannah repositions her and continues walking past us, barely sparing me a glance.

I still have to prove myself not only to Sedona, but her entire family. As uncomfortable as it is, I duck into the waiting area and take a chair away from the rest of them. They talk and reassure Austin that it's all going to be okay, and I try to take their confidence into my own psyche.

Palmer finds her way over to me and crawls onto the chair next to me before placing her hand in mine. She has no idea what's going on with her mom right now, but I want to hold her close because she's part of Sedona and me together. We made her, and she's perfect. Just like I know Sedona and I will be again.

NINE

Sedona

Having emergency surgery puts a lot of things in perspective. As I lie in the hospital bed, Holly and Austin are tucked in the corner with their newborn daughter, Harper, my thoughts drift back to when they told me I was going in for a C-section. That Harper was in distress and they needed to get her out.

Austin and Holly hugged and decided she'd be the one to stay with me. I saw the tug-of-war in Austin's eyes. Sure, his primary concern was Harper, but his second was me. How fast things can change and become beyond your control.

I felt the fear too. What if something happened to me? What would happen to Palmer? Sure, my family would raise her, but Jamison would have a right to her too.

I watch them smile and nuzzle Harper closer. Holly's tears only controllable for short stints. It takes me back to when I delivered Palmer and it was Phoenix holding my hand, the two of us cuddled in the twin-size hospital bed, pointing out every Bailey characteristic on my daughter's face, acting as if her fair skin and narrow nose weren't clear signs of the Ferguson genes. As if I had somehow immaculately birthed a baby with no father.

For the past eighteen months, I've pushed the topic of her father as far as I could, never considering what would happen to Palmer if something happened to me. Now Jamison is here, in Lake Starlight, asking to be a part of her life. I can't very well shut the door in his face. My siblings have their own lives. It's time that I address the fact that he's going to be a part of ours.

The nurse comes in and interrupts my thoughts, wanting to take Harper for some tests. Holly follows, but Austin walks over to my bedside.

"You ready for visitors?" he asks. "You had a lot of people scared."

"Could you have someone bring Palmer to me?"

He nods, squeezes my hand, and leaves the room.

A few minutes later, Grandma Dori steps into the room with Palmer.

Mommy. She smiles, but I can tell she's confused as to why I'm in this bed.

Grandma Dori helps Palmer crawl up onto the bed. I tuck her to my side, trying to steer clear of my stitches. I have no idea how I'm going to get through this recovery while chasing after her.

Grandma Dori sits in a chair by the bedside. "How are you, dear?"

"I'm good. Not too sore yet since all the drugs are flowing through my system still. I'll be here for three days. I need to find someone to take care of Palmer, then even when I get home, I'll have restrictions."

I hate being unable to care for my own child. I'm happy

I helped Austin and Holly have another baby, but I didn't realize I'd be in this position. I assumed my physical recovery would be like it was after Palmer, but without the sleepless nights.

Grandma Dori pats my hand. "I'll help you, and as for Palmer, she can stay with me."

"With you?" I raise my eyebrows.

Palmer rests her head on my chest and wraps her arm around me. From the increasing weight of her body on me, I'm positive she's falling asleep.

"Yes, Sedona, I can take care of a child. I had a son, and who do you think helped your mother wrangle you all?"

"I didn't mean to offend you, but will the retirement community even allow Palmer to stay there?" One night is one thing, three is a whole other. Plus, Grandma doesn't drive anymore, which means Palmer will be riding in Grandma's Caddy with Ethel behind the wheel. What am I thinking? I need a quick excuse to get out of this situation. "Thanks for the offer, but Palmer doesn't sleep well in other places. I'll just ask Kingston and Stella to come stay with her at our house. But I'd really appreciate it if once I'm discharged, you could come over and help me during the day. Maybe take her to the park and stuff."

Her smile says I've won her over enough. I doubt she really wanted Palmer at night anyway. "Perfect. I'll get your apartment situated."

I wave her off. "Oh no, I'm fine."

"Nonsense." She pats my hand again. "There's someone who really wants to see you."

"No." I shake my head. "I'm not ready."

But she disappears out the door, not listening. No real surprise there.

I sigh. Staring at Palmer's sleeping body next to me, I

run my hand over her dark hair and down her chubby arms. She's never been away from me for even one night. I have no idea how she's going to handle the separation.

A large figure fills the doorway in my peripheral and my heart gallops. I glance up, and he rushes into the room as if I granted him permission.

"Damn it, Sedona, I was so scared." He comes to the other side of the bed, opposite Palmer. His calloused palm slides into my hand and he covers the back of my hand with his other one, sandwiching mine between both of his. A shiver runs up my arm. "Yer good? Everything's good?" His gaze falls down my body, inspecting every inch.

"I'm fine."

"Did you have a C-section with Palmer?" His eyes concentrate on the area of my incision underneath my hospital gown.

"No. I had her vaginally."

He nods a few times, fast, as if he's really concerned. His hands squeeze mine. "I'm just so happy yer all right. I was so scared."

I'm not sure what to do with his fearful expression. There's so much animosity living inside me that my first reaction is to ask him why he cares now when he didn't care all these months we've been apart. But my anger isn't going to help Palmer, so I nod. "I'll be fine, but you should know a few things."

"Okay." His blue eyes are wide and attentive.

"I'm here for three days. I'm hoping to get out sooner, but I don't know if that will happen. Then once I'm discharged, I'll have some restrictions—I can't drive for two weeks, I'll only be able to go up the stairs once a day, I can't lift anything heavy." When I pause, his mouth opens. I'm sure it's to say he'll pick up the slack, and I hate the small part of me that feels bad I'm about to crush that hopeful expression on his face. "I'm going to ask Kingston and Stella to watch Palmer while I'm in here. She's most familiar with them."

His hand leaves mine to push through his hair. "Yeah, of course." His vision darts to her before coming back to me.

"Jamison—"

He shakes his head. "I get it. I do. Do you think they'll let me see her?"

I inhale a deep breath. There's a longing in his eyes that I've yet to see from him since he's popped back into our lives. He's gotten a small taste of her and he's concerned I'm stripping that away from him.

"I'll make sure of it." The words are hard to get out, but Palmer deserves to know her dad.

He blows out a breath and Palmer stirs in my arms.

"Maybe you can have her during the day. Stella works at her practice and Kingston might have a shift at the fire department."

"Is he not smoke jumping anymore?" he asks.

Questions like that make me realize how much he's missed. "No. He stopped because he wants to be with Stella. The smoke jumping just took him away for too long at a time."

"So he's just working in Anchorage now?"

I nod. "Yeah. But he's twenty-four hours on and forty-eight hours off."

"Okay." He nods and thinks of his next words, seeming unsure but then blurts them out. "Can I help you after you get home?"

That would be the most logical option, but I'm not stupid. The small fluttering in my stomach when I'm in Jamison's presence is already alive and taking care of someone can be intimate especially after having a baby. "I don't think that's a good idea. But we can plan days you can come and see Palmer."

His gaze moves to her as though he's figuring out how to play this. Eventually, he nods and clears his throat. "There're a lot of people who want to see you." Standing, he steps away from the bed.

How is it that I feel like the bad guy here?

"Can you take her with you? I'm going to talk to Kingston." I know telling him that Jamison will be over to visit with Palmer won't be the most pleasant conversation.

"Really?" His eyes sparkle and the corners of his mouth turn up. "Sure."

Palmer transfers easier than I prefer, finding her favorite position over his chest. Damn, he looks good with her. Too good. Edible kind of good. That's exactly why he cannot help me next week.

"I'll be in the waiting room," he says.

"Can I just kiss her quick?"

He nods and bends down, leaning her toward me. I get a whiff of his scent, one that's all man. The one I associate with losing my virginity, lazy Sunday mornings in New York City, long nights that ended with me cuddling into him in a cab, slow dancing at weddings. Jamison's scent has always been like being wrapped in a warm blanket in front of a fireplace.

And I realize in this moment, I miss that.

I kiss Palmer's forehead and close my eyes, my mind drifting to once upon a time.

"I'm really glad yer good," he says at the door, leaving me before I can respond.

If someone would've asked me years ago if I ever thought Jamison and I could be in a room together and be so uncomfortable with each other, I would've said they were crazy.

A few minutes later, Kingston comes in and kisses my cheek before falling into a chair at my bedside. He gives me a sad sort of smile. "Don't worry. We worked out the schedule in the waiting room."

"What?"

"Palmer will stay with Stella and me during the night, then go to Phoenix or Brooklyn's during the day. Juno said she can take a day off if needed. I have to work tomorrow, then I'm done for forty-eight. I just have to coach the Thunderdogs, but Palmer loves coming with me. I'll bring Maverick, and he can—"

I put up my hand. "You've all figured out a schedule without consulting me?"

He tilts his head, forehead creased.

Can I really blame them? My family has helped me so much since I returned a hot pregnant mess. I'm appreciative, but at the same time, I hate that they *know* they're going to have to step in and help me. Have I really abdicated the responsibility of making decisions and taking care of myself? If Jamison weren't here, would I think twice about their plans? Allow them to keep treating me like the baby of the family who always needs a helping hand?

"I'd like Jamison to see her."

He guffaws.

"I'm serious, Kingston. He's here and Palmer deserves to know her father."

He rolls his eyes, his big frame taking up so much space in the room. The chip on his shoulder takes up even more. "Why? So she can become attached to him before he leaves her?"

I blow out a breath. "At this point, I don't have a choice.

He's her father, and whether we all like it or not, he has rights. He could take me to court if he wanted to. I'd rather do this slowly on my terms. Ease Palmer into it."

"Ease her into it." He shakes his head. "She's plastered to his chest right now."

"Maybe she has some innate understanding that he's her father." I shrug. "She deserves to have her father in her life."

He sits up ramrod-straight. "You're serious?"

I nod.

"This is going to end in disaster," he says, shaking his head.

"Please don't give him a hard time. Meet him at a park or at the house or go on a walk. I don't know, just keep things civil in front of Palmer."

He stands. "It's your life, your heart. You've always been too forgiving though, so no promises about not giving him a hard time."

"Thanks for making this easier on me," I say with sarcasm.

He stares at me long and hard. Kingston and Stella know better than anyone how hard it was for me when I returned home from New York. The postpartum depression that plagued me after I had Palmer. How much I missed Jamison. I can't fault King for having bad feelings toward him, especially when he doesn't have the good memories that I do. Like that time Jamison showed up on my doorstep when he got into the MLS.

TEN

Sedona

Twenty-one years old

It was my last year of school and my first year in my own apartment, and the kitchen, dining room, and bedroom were all one room. Small but efficient. It was enough for me.

On the way home, I stop to pick up pizza because I have an article to write for the paper. It's an ongoing series about hot places to visit in the city on a budget. Last week, I scoped out numerous coffee houses that were good places to study. I rated them, and although I have most of the research done, I've been procrastinating writing the actual article.

Just as I sit down with my laptop and pizza at my dining table for two, a knock sounds on the door. A few years ago, it would have startled me since I'm not expecting anyone, but I've come to enjoy New York. I don't fear the unknown of big cities anymore.

I rise on my tiptoes to peer through my peephole, and

all that's there is a bouquet of ranunculus—the peach and apricot ones I love so much. Only a few people know they're my favorite.

"Who is it?" I ask, my eyes not straying from the peephole.

"Flower delivery," a man says in a muffled voice.

I'd wonder how he got buzzed into the building, but sadly I know the answer. Too many times, I've seen people allow others to come into the building without even asking them what they're doing there.

I unlock the door and swing it open. The man holding the flowers lowers them, but he didn't have to for me to know who he is. I memorized those hands years ago, lying on a blanket under the stars in Lake Starlight.

"Jamie!" I say, my heart floating out of my chest and right into his capable hands as if no time has passed. But it's been four years since I've laid eyes on him in person and not through a television screen.

"Surprise!" he says, his smile wide and welcoming, his arms open and inviting.

It doesn't take but a second before I'm rushing into his arms, wrapping my own around his shoulders and allowing him to lift me off the ground.

"You still smell so damn good, lass," he says, his accent making my skin tingle.

"Like sweat and pizza?" I laugh, inhaling him and the familiar scent that is Jamison.

"No. You smell delicious."

Tingles scatter along my flesh. "I can't believe you're here."

He lowers me and hands me the flowers.

It's then I see the suitcase and duffel bag at his feet. "What are you doing here?"

"Hear me out," he says, grabbing his luggage and stepping inside my apartment that suddenly feels the homiest it has since I moved in.

I drag him by his hand to the couch. His lips look delectable, his body harder than when I last saw it. Watching his games and seeing pictures of him on Instagram, I noticed how he's morphed into manhood with thicker muscles, wider shoulders, and steel calves, but those pictures didn't prepare me for Jamison Ferguson live and in person.

"I got a position on the New York Storm."

"A US team? You're not playing in Scotland anymore?"

He shakes his head. "I didn't want to say anything until it was for sure. I had this whole idea to surprise you." He bites the side of his lips, and I know him well enough to know that he wants my reassurance that it was the right decision.

"I'm so happy you're here." I throw myself at him, and he positions me so I'm over his lap. Such a familiar place.

After we said goodbye our senior year, we promised visits that never happened. Although there were calls and text messages exchanged, we were both so busy, maintaining a relationship was impossible, especially with him being in a different time zone and traveling so much. We decided not to do a long distance relationship. It was an incredibly hard realization to come to, and I felt the loss of him for a very long time. I've never seen him in a picture with a woman that would suggest he moved on, and I've never asked because I don't really want to know. I've gone on a few dates, but nothing ever felt like this, like it does right now.

"Am I... I mean, is there someone..."

I smash my lips to his, answering his question. His hand

slides to the back of my head, keeping me there as his tongue glides effortlessly into my mouth. God, I missed this... him... us. It always feels so right when we're together. He draws our kiss to a close and I shift so that I'm straddling him.

"That's a no, I take it." He grins.

I nod, my gaze falling to his lips. His fingers run along the skin between my shirt and yoga pants, goose bumps skittering along their path. "So you're here permanently now?"

He nods. "Except for traveling for games. New York City is my new home."

I close my eyes and inhale a deep breath. He tucks a strand of hair that's fallen loose from my ponytail behind my ear, then he pulls out the elastic band. My long dark strands fall down over one of my shoulders.

"Yer so gorgeous. My imaginings of what this moment would be weren't even close to what I'm feeling right now."

"I know what you mean." My body hums for his touch. For the exploration of his lips and his fingertips over my flesh. My core aches to feel him inside me.

His hands slide higher up my back and I sink down farther into his lap, feeling how hard he is under his track pants. "Yer so soft."

"You're so hard," I say, my fingers gliding down the row of abs I feel beneath his T-shirt.

"Are we moving too fast?" he asks, his hands inching up along my sides, waiting patiently to touch my breasts.

"I don't think so." I grab the hem of his shirt and pull up. His hands leave my body briefly so I can shed the fabric from his body.

And I was right. A rippled, lean, muscular body resides underneath the thin fabric. I lick my lips.

"Like what you see, lass?" he asks, his Adam's apple bobbing up and down.

I nod. "You've grown up."

He takes the hem of my shirt between his thumb and forefinger and raises it off my chest.

"I should shower," I say.

He shakes his head, relieving me of my sports bra, which isn't exactly the sexiest undergarment ever. But his eyes are fixated on my breasts and his tongue slides out and over his bottom lip, so he must like what he sees.

The hunger smoldering in his eyes eats away any reservations of what it will be like now that we're adults. Ten minutes ago, I didn't think I'd be having sex with my ex today, but it's not too fast. Not for us. He was my first and only. Although I'm out of practice, he's Jamie.

He kisses my collarbone, his lips moving up my neck, across my jaw. I grind down on his length, my hips on autopilot—like in high school, when we'd dry hump after everyone was in bed or out of the house.

When I fall forward, my pebbled nipples run over the hard warmth of his chest and my core tightens, screaming for release. As though he understands, he lifts me with him, rising from the couch and walking the five feet to my bed. He stares at me with hunger in his eyes.

"Yer too thin," he says.

I inch my head back. "Excuse me?"

"Are you eating?"

"If this is your way of romancing me, it's not working." I grab the comforter and cover myself.

He lifts it off my body. "Yer beautiful. I'm just worried I'm going to hurt you now."

"Hurt me? Maybe we just shouldn't talk." I climb to my knees.

"I'm scared to be on top. I don't wanna crush you." He nibbles on his lip.

I start laughing. Of course, this is us. The first time we had sex, we went through five condoms before we had it on right. Both of our heads bent down, examining the latex over his shaft, paranoid I'd get pregnant. The less-than-stellar blow jobs I gave him until I learned what made him tick. The fact that he had no idea what he was doing between my legs, but lucky for him, I'm a great teacher.

We explored one another's bodies late at night when Austin was upstairs watching television, or on lazy spring days when we'd pretend to go swimming at the pond. Somewhere between the steamy make-out sessions and heavy petting, there was always laughter.

I place my hands on his chest and lay him on his back, straddling him. "Problem solved."

His hands steady on my hips. "You always were a great problem-solver."

With a grin, I rock forward. He raises his hips off the mattress, matching my pace. Even through the thin fabric of my yoga pants and his track pants, my clit screams for more.

"How did I think my life was good until I got here?" His hands slide up my ribcage and take my breasts into his palms. "Being here, right now, feels like I just made it to the World Cup."

His words, always so on point, make me blush. I feel so desired and dare I say loved. Jamison's never made me feel anything other than gorgeous. As though I was made to be his.

"How have we gone so long without us?" I ask in a breathy whisper. I rise off him to pull down his track pants and shed my yoga pants. "Do you have a condom?"

Please say yes.

"Side of the duffel bag," he says.

I unzip it and pull out a box still in the plastic bag from the corner drug store. I tap it against my lips, looking at him. "Felt lucky today?"

He chuckles—probably since I'm naked while asking. He didn't have to assume. He knew that if we were both single, we wouldn't be able to keep our hands off each other.

"Yeah, okay." I drop the plastic bag as I walk back to him, opening up the box and pulling out a strip before tearing one off.

"Yer the problem-solver and I'm the planner. It's how we work so well together."

I nod. "Very true."

And he's so right. Jamison has had his life planned out since he was fourteen. Checkpoints along the way to make his dream come true. I wonder how long he's been planning this move to New York. Questions for later.

I pull back his foreskin and roll the condom down his rigid length.

He sucks in a breath as though having my hands on him is too much. "Now get yer arse on top of me. I can't wait to be inside you."

I straddle him then arrange him at my entrance. As soon as I sink down, we both groan.

If I thought we'd take it slow, that I'd rock and tease him while we lovingly stared into each other's eyes, I was completely wrong.

I plant my palms on his muscular chest, his fingertips digging into my hips. Our speed increases with every thrust, sweat slicking our bodies and our mouths tangled in a frenzied kiss. Our hands grip and grope as if we're afraid we're in a dream and about to wake up.

"I'm never leaving you again," he says and flips me on my back, locking my hands above my head.

His weight is heavier than I remember, but I love it all the same. He slides back inside me, and I wrap my legs around his waist.

We find that rhythm we mastered as kids, as though it's as easy as riding a bike. Our breathing is labored, curses and praise for one another coming out in a tangle. My body races toward the cliff's edge. Jamison can still tell when I'm there because a devilish smirk crosses his lips. He thrusts over and over, tilting my hips up with his hands on my ass. Then I'm falling, plummeting into an abyss as I clench around him. All that built-up sexual frustration bursts apart in a glorious orgasm my body has ached for.

"Almost there," he whispers, his pace still punishing.

He pumps into me twice more and stills, gazing at me with love in his eyes.

A year later, I moved in with him.

ELEVEN

Jamison

I'm not sure I understood what I'd feel when I saw Palmer the first time. Would I have immediate love for my daughter, or would she feel like a stranger? But the minute I saw her, I fell in love with her and felt even more regret for missing her first eighteen months of life. So as I transfer her sleeping body to Kingston, the urge to erase that pain with alcohol is a sharp reminder of why I lost it all.

After the rest of the Baileys leave the hospital, Phoenix lingers. I bet she stays with Sedona for all three nights. She's going to be my biggest roadblock to winning over Sedona.

"Please feel free to go on with your life now," she snips.

"I was going to stay and keep her company," I say.

She rolls her eyes and huffs. "Yeah, sorry, buddy, that's my job now."

Phoenix and I haven't always seen eye to eye. I never imagined dating a twin would be so hard. From day one of being with Sedona, it's proved a challenge. Phoenix is the alpha dog and likes to dictate what Sedona should do with her life. I'm guessing their relationship has always been that way because it took years away from Phoenix before Sedona stopped letting her railroad her into everything.

"I get that you hate me—"

She's quick to laugh. "Hate is a mild way of stating my feelings for you." She crosses her arms.

It's a strange sensation to fight with someone who looks exactly like the person you love. "Fine. You can loathe me or whatever level of hatred you have for me, that's your right, but let Sedona figure this out on her own. Let her decide whether she wants to give us another chance."

"Another chance? Are you delusional? You left her."

"Technically, she walked out on me."

"Because you were a drunk! Partying all the time while she was preparing to be a mother. She had no choice because you were such a mess over losing your dream."

A few nurses side-eye us while they walk by.

"Yeah, I fucked up. I think you've had more than your fair share of fuck-ups over the years."

I'm not going to bother asking her what would happen if she suddenly lost her voice and couldn't sell a record to save her life. What she would do doesn't matter. The fact is, losing my dream crushed me, and yeah, I made the wrong choice. A lot of wrong choices in fact. And now I have to own them.

"Why were you gone so long? I mean, you could have come sooner. Reached out?"

I eye Griffin and Maverick sitting outside on a bench, hoping they're waiting for Phoenix so I can go see Sedona. "I had to make sure I was stable and wouldn't make the same mistake again. If I came too early and I wasn't prepared to handle everything... I don't expect you to understand."

Another roll of her eyes. "You could still fuck this up—again. Believe me, if that happens, I won't be taking a backseat. None of us will."

I'm surprised it's taken her this long to threaten me. Phoenix does nothing half-assed.

"Fine. If I fuck up again, you get the first punch."

"With brass knuckles," she says.

"Sure, brass knuckles and all."

She shakes her head and steadies her gaze on me. "Stop trying to make this a joke."

I raise both hands. "I'm not joking. I'm serious. If I fuck this up, you're welcome to beat me to a bloody pulp, okay?" I step forward, lowering my voice. "But, Phoenix, I'll warn you now, I'm not going anywhere. I'm here to win my family back. So you can try to interfere and be the annoying bee in your sister's ear, but a love like ours doesn't disappear after one fuck-up. Even a giant one like mine. I guarantee she still loves me. I wasn't in the right frame of mind when I let her leave me, but I am now. And things are going to be very different. You can either accept that or not. I'm trying to prove myself to you all but there are only two people I really care about making amends to, and one of them is lying in the hospital and the other one is wondering who the hell her daddy is. So you can take yer threats and shove them up yer arse." I step back and stuff my hands in my pockets.

To my surprise, Phoenix says nothing, but her seething eyes speak volumes. I'm not backing down though. From what I can tell, it'll be her and Kingston standing as a united front, trying to keep me from Sedona. If I stand firm and make them see how important this is to me, maybe they'll eventually back off.

The sliding doors of the hospital open, Maverick

standing there. "Dad said we have to go. The plane is ready."

Phoenix exhales, staring long and hard at me. "I have to go to LA for a meeting with my record label." She pokes me in the chest. "I'm stopping on the way back to buy a pair of brass knuckles, so don't fuck it up." She twirls around and stomps away from me. "Coming, sweetie," she say in a sweet-as-pie voice.

Maverick groans. "Phoenix, you can't call me that anymore."

She rests her arm over her stepson's shoulders. "Sorry, I forgot. Dude a better option?"

Maverick groans again and Phoenix laughs as if she can change her mood with the flick of a switch. But then she glances over her shoulder to give me a death stare.

I turn around and head to the hospital gift shop, happy to finally be alone with Sedona for as long as she'll allow me.

TURNS out there's a lot of sleeping after you have a baby, plus she's on pain pills, so I'm not sure she even knows I'm in the chair next to her.

As I watch deliveries of flowers and balloons being taken to other rooms, Sedona's room remains bare except for the snacks and magazines I gave her. I suppose that's normal since she's not going home with a baby.

I flick through the television to find anything other than some raunchy talk show about who's the daddy or a court show where two people can't be civilized enough to handle their affairs off-air and choose instead to bring their grievances in front of a judge for all the world to see.

Holly stands in the doorway, appearing alarmed to find me. I drop my feet from the chair I slid in front of me to stretch out.

"I didn't think you'd be here. I thought everyone left." She hovers at the door.

"They did. I stayed."

A small smile creases her lips. "I just wanted to check on her. We're in a room down the hall with Harper. We should be released tomorrow though. She's perfectly healthy." She steps into the room hesitantly as if there's a live wire at her feet.

"Sedona's pretty out of it. The nurse just gave her a dose of pain pills and she's been asleep ever since."

Resting her back on the wall, Holly crosses her ankles. "Yeah, I slept almost an entire day afterward. Lucky for me, I had Austin to help with Easton."

I nod, understanding her sly way of ridiculing the fact that I wasn't here to help Sedona. "I can't take back what happened."

She holds up her hand. "I know. I didn't mean like that."

I raise my eyebrows.

"Okay, maybe a little, but it sounded much worse out loud than it did in my head. Listen." She breaks the distance. "You know this family. You've known them longer than me."

Yeah, for some reason, Holly is still more Principal Radcliffe in my mind than someone who will hopefully be my sister-in-law one day.

"They're tight, and the mistake you made was huge. You're up against a lot, but I also think she still loves you."

I inch forward as though she's about to let me in on a secret.

"And I would never argue with the heart. It wins every time. It's not always right, but it's too powerful for the mind to convince otherwise. The heart takes all rational thoughts and beliefs and throws them in a dumpster. All I ask of you is to make sure, because the woman in that bed just gave me the best gift anyone ever could." A tear trickles down her cheek and she swipes it, shaking her head as if she still can't believe how lucky she is. "I mean, I can never pay her back but... I don't want to be a boulder in the way of her getting what she wants. I think there's enough of those people lined up between you two." She fixes her gaze on Sedona's sleeping form. "She's special and deserves to be treated as such."

"I know."

She smiles. "I'm really proud of you for going to rehab and getting your life in order."

I chuckle. Always the principal. I remember when she had every senior visit her during the first year she was a principal so she could ask about our life plans and help us chart a course. From the way she's talking to me, she must remember what I told her. God knows I've never forgotten. Soccer and Sedona are still my goal, even if the soccer part is going to be different than I imagined. "Thanks."

"I'm serious, Jamison. It's something to be proud of. A lot of people lose the battle."

"I'm not sure my fight will ever be over."

She nods. "Probably not, but I think you're moving in the right direction."

We look at Sedona peacefully sleeping. What I wouldn't do to slide into that bed and hold her. "I think so too."

She gives my shoulder a squeeze and leaves the room. I lean back in my chair, dozing for I don't know how long until I try to change position and the arm on the chair forbids movement, so I sit up, stretching my neck and back.

Sedona's staring at me with her untouched dinner tray in front of her.

I sit up straight, blinking my eyes to fully awake. "What time is it?"

"Six," she says. "Why are you here?"

"I wasn't gonna leave you alone."

"I'm not. Holly and Austin are here."

"Down the hall."

She stares at me for a moment, probably wondering how I'd know that.

"I brought you some magazines and your favorite snacks."

She glances at them on the windowsill. "Thanks. I'm fully capable of staying here by myself."

"I know yer *capable,* but that doesn't mean you *should.* I got a deck of cards. Want to play Rummy?" I grab them from the table where I was playing Solitaire earlier.

"Jamison," she sighs.

"Come on, I'm not asking for much. Just for you to let me help you through this. I'll be your slave. What do you want? Me to feed you? A sponge bath? It's a sacrifice I'm willing to make."

She laughs, then grips her stomach. "Don't make me laugh."

But it's such a beautiful sound. "I'm here as a friend, I promise."

She looks at me skeptically. "No, you're not, but I need a distraction from not having Palmer, so fine. But we're playing Hearts, not Rummy."

"Deal."

During my ankle surgeries and recovery, we mastered

every card game two people could play. She was there for me during my time in a hospital bed and I'll be here for her. I liked it a lot better when it was me in that bed though.

"And hand me the Doritos. I cannot eat this food."

I snag the chocolate pudding while she pushes away her tray.

"Oh, good catch. I'll have that." She smiles and grabs the pudding out of my hands.

It's amazing how it seems like nothing has changed except for the huge reality that we share a daughter now. All my dreams are there, just out of my reach. I don't hold them all in my hand just yet though. Yet being the keyword.

TWELVE

Sedona

I foolishly allowed Jamison to stay the night at the hospital. And now he's on one side of me with the nurse on the other, helping me to stand. The doctor is insisting that I get up and walk by the end of the day.

"Just a few steps and then we'll get you in the wheelchair. You and Jamison can work on it little by little."

"How are you on a first-name basis with him?" I ask the nurse, who beams at Jamison.

"He had a delivery of donuts brought to us this morning."

Another member of the Jamison Ferguson fan club. Wonderful.

"You work fast," I mumble in his direction.

After I take the few steps to the wheelchair, my lower abdomen feels as if it's on fire. This is definitely harder than after I had Palmer.

"Good job, Sedona," she says. "Now don't go too fast with her, Jamison." She laughs.

I want to put my finger in my throat and gag like a thirteen-year-old.

"Thanks, Katrina," he says, and I swear he's laying his Scottish accent on thick.

"Have her back by twelve for lunch and pain pills."

"Where are we going?" I ask.

"It's a surprise," he says and wheels me slowly down the hallway.

We pass all the rooms with new moms inside. What a great place to work. Everyone's so happy. Even the day I had Palmer was the happiest day of my life. I missed Jamison—this Jamison, who treats me like his most cherished possession—but I had my family.

He rolls us onto the elevator and stays at my back, saying nothing. He remains silent, but I hear his phone vibrate in his pocket. I haven't had the nerve to ask him about the coaching jobs he's applied for. I'm trying to keep our relationship on a course where we can be great parents to Palmer. A team. If he ends up coaching, he'll have an off season. We'll figure out the time apart.

He wheels me into the courtyard and the sun warms my face. I tilt my head back to soak up as much as I can get.

"Thank you," I say.

He wraps a blanket over my legs and another one over my shoulders. "It's colder than I thought."

Rolling me up to a table, I spot another one farther down where a woman is crying. Other people surround her, trying to console her. While the baby floor is brimming with happiness, many other parts of this building aren't as optimistic.

"Now, hold up, I'll be right back," Jamison says and walks back inside the hospital.

I take the opportunity to close my eyes and enjoy the

sun on my face. It isn't until I hear commotion from the table next to us that I open my eyes to find Jamison walking in with Palmer in his arms.

"Oh, how sweet," one woman says.

How did he manage to get someone to drop off Palmer here?

Palmer squirms to get out of his hold, but Jamison holds her tight until he can place the diaper bag on the table and gently place her on my lap. Her arms go around my neck and tears free fall down my face now that she's with me again.

Jamison sits in the chair across from us, smiling. I have to give him credit—the man still knows what I need more than I do.

Palmer leans back, and I reposition her legs not to dig into my incision. There's a question in her eyes. *Sad?*

No, happy.

Her little eyebrows draw down. *Cry.*

Happy tears. I missed you.

She smiles and it's like the sun warming my chest. It's the best thing in the world.

Her fingers rise again. *I slept at Uncle and Auntie.*

Did you have fun?

Her smile says she did. *Yes.* She looks over her shoulder at Jamison and back at me. *Friend?*

Jamison looks away toward the building. A pang of guilt rises in me, and *I shake my head.* She looks at him again, as though she knows and understands what I'm about to tell her. But there's no possible way she can.

Who?

I study Jamison. He glances our way again, and if I'm reading him right, he can't bear for me to say he's just a friend. He wants her to know. After last night, I know that the Jamison I fell in love with is still in there. I won't allow myself to love him again, but my daughter can.

"I think it's time. Are you ready?" I ask him.

Palmer puts her hand on my face and turns me to face her. She doesn't like when she sees lips moving and no one signs.

He straightens. It's cute the way he looks nervous and like he's preparing himself for an important interview or something. And that's how I know I'm making the right choice.

Not friend. Daddy.

Her eyes widen. *Me?*

I inhale a deep breath and my eyes are full to the brim with tears. It has to be the hormones. *Yours.* I point at her.

She doesn't immediately smile like I thought she would. She throws herself at me. I wince a bit because of my incision but allow her arms to wrap so tight around my neck that I might suffocate. Then she scurries off my lap until her feet find the pavement.

Moving to the other chair, she climbs onto Jamison's lap with his help. He positions her so I can see what she signs too. It's a show of respect. Someone without a deaf family member probably wouldn't have even thought of it.

My daddy?

Jamison nods and his jaw clenches. His Adam's apple bobs with a deep swallow.

Palmer hugs him. I gasp when his eyes close and tears drip down his cheeks.

She draws back. *Sad?*

He shakes his head with a small chuckle.

Tears?

Happy tears.

Then she hugs him again, and Jamison mouths thank you to me.

So much for baby steps.

THREE DAYS LATER, I'm finally released. Everyone was unavailable, so I'm left with Ethel and Grandma driving me back to my apartment. Palmer is with Harley, but no one expected her to pack all their kids into the car to pick me up.

I wait in my hospital room, my bags packed, eager to be with Palmer again. But I'm not prepared when Jamison steps into the doorway. "What are you doing here?"

"I'm your chauffeur."

"I thought Grandma Dori and Ethel were coming?"

He grabs my bag and a nurse comes in with my discharge papers. "Yeah, Ethel is sick, so here I am. It's not too much of a disappointment, is it?"

I shrug and focus on the nurse. She's too busy smiling at Jamison. I know he's good-looking. I had to fight women off all the time when we were together, but in my back pocket, I always had the security that he was mine. Now he's not, and jealousy slaps me hard across the face.

He clears his throat and the nurse smiles, straightening the papers on her desk. As if she wasn't just ogling him. The hospital is way too small for everyone to not know the situation here. I carried my brother and his wife's baby, and Jamison is *my* baby daddy.

The nurse gives me all the instructions and my list of restrictions.

Jamison clarifies with her about the stairs. "Once a day?"

The nurse nods. "Once up and once down, that's it."

He nods as though he's the one in charge. He won't be near me except to get Palmer, and honestly, these are just guidelines. Things they have to tell women for insurance reasons. Surely, I'll be fine. I mean, most women have to go home and care for a baby. I just have an eighteen-month-old sweet little girl who listens to her mother.

After we complete all the discharge paperwork, I get myself into the wheelchair and Jamison asks the dreaded question about sex.

"Six weeks, huh?" Jamison asks and gives me a look of disbelief.

I'm sure we're both thinking that if he had been around after Palmer, we couldn't have waited that long. We've had sex through head colds, recovery from two ankle surgeries, and while I was pregnant—until he was drinking too much.

"Six weeks. You'll have your doctor's appointment at week two to check things out. I'm sure your doctor can tell you more than me." The nurse hands me off to an orderly by the elevator. "Good luck, Sedona. Bye, Jamison."

She's off and we're in the elevator with a new person. A man, thankfully. Someone who hopefully won't eye Jamison as if he's a prized bull.

I wait patiently as Jamison pulls his car around, but when it stops in the circle drive, I arch my eyebrows. He climbs out of the two-door Camaro and rounds the back of the car.

I allow him to help me to the car. "You rented this for Alaska?"

"I figure it's spring. Don't have to worry about the snow."

He opens up the passenger door and I ease down into

the seat, which isn't easy when your stomach is stitched together.

After the orderly gives Jamison the rest of my stuff, he shoves it in the trunk. Neither of us had a car in New York, so I never gave much thought to his preference of car. But this is the most impractical thing he could have rented. I glance down as he shifts it into first gear. A stick shift? Seriously?

As we drive out of the hospital parking lot, I grow irritated. Maybe it's that he's sexy when he drives a stick and I don't want to admit it to myself.

"You do know that Palmer will never ride in this?"

At a red light, he glances to me with confusion in his eyes.

"It's too dangerous." I glance behind me. "Your back seat isn't big enough and—"

The smile that warmed his face when he pulled up outside the hospital turns into a guilty expression and he drags his eyes back to the road. "Yeah. I wasn't thinking."

The pang of guilt for delivering my message rudely shouldn't bother me. What do I care if I offended him? Any father would know this car isn't practical—not in Alaska and not for an eighteen-month-old girl. And he would've thought of it on his own if... I stop my train of thought. I can't let the anger that's yet to dissipate toward him take over.

"It's just that—"

He holds up his hand. "I got it. I'll switch it out."

"I didn't mean—"

"It's fine."

I sulk down in the seat, and we drive the rest of the way in silence. By the time we reach my apartment and park along the curb, I'm itching to get out of such close proximity with him. He helps me out of the car, which is a complete embarrassment because of how painful it is to get out of his car.

"Thank you for bringing me home," I say once my feet land on the sidewalk.

His eyes lock with mine. "I'm sorry."

"No, I shouldn't have—"

"You should have. You have every right. Our daughter's safety is the number one concern. I'm just embarrassed that I didn't think about it myself. Do you think I'll ever have those instincts? What if I'm just a shit dad?" He blows out a breath and pushes his hand through his hair.

Oh no, this is not how it was supposed to go. I'm supposed to hate the man in front of me. I'm not the person who should boost up his self-esteem about being a dad. Because I had all those doubts once too, but I dealt with them on my own because he wasn't anywhere to be found.

"I think you're a new dad and I've been at this for eighteen months. Don't beat yourself up just because you picked the wrong car at the rental place."

He nods. "Thanks. You shouldn't have to make me feel better."

I huff. "Well, I might still be mad at you, but I'm not a bitch either. Parenthood is hard. No one promised it was easy. You should know that too."

"I'll do better. I promise." He disappears to the back of the car before I have the opportunity to say anything else.

Which is probably for the best. I don't want to be the person who assures him he'll be a great dad. With the way he dedicates himself to something he loves, I know he will. Maybe that scares me too. Like he's threatening the bubble I've put Palmer and myself in. I'm not sure I want to make room for him. Just the thought of holidays without her grips my heart as if the Incredible Hulk is squeezing it.

"Let's get you settled." He holds my bags in one hand and he waits for me to slowly walk to my apartment, following.

But I can't depend on Jamison to have my back. I made that mistake once already.

THIRTEEN

Jamison

I'm on my way to the rental place when my phone dings in the center console. All I catch is 911, so I pull over to the side of the road and pick it up.

It's an unknown number, but it's an Alaska area code.

Unknown Number: 911. *Sedona needs help and needs a new breast pump. Hers is broken.*

I stare at the words, trying to process who's sending this to me. The phone vibrates in my hand and another text message pops up.

Unknown Number: *Don't skimp on the price. Imagine a suction on your penis, would you go cheap? I think not.*

What the fuck? I stare at the message for some clue as to who this is, but I don't have enough time to figure it out because they message again.

Unknown Number: *Go to the baby store in town, Jamison. Ask for a breast pump. Get over to Sedona's. Are these instructions simple enough?*

I look around as if whoever the person is can see me sitting idle on the side of the road. What the hell? But Dori told me she'd convey to me anything Sedona asked her for, so it must be her, I guess. I put the car in drive and head back toward downtown Lake Starlight.

Ten minutes later, I park in the public parking lot and head inside Sweet Home Baby Boutique. It's not until the door chimes and Mrs. Bennington peeks out of the back room that my shoulders sink. Mrs. Bennington was the next-door neighbor of my host family senior year.

After I graduated, my host family moved to Arizona to be near their son but running into Mrs. Bennington feels just as bad as hearing from Georgie. Part of me thinks I should leave and put on those pads men use for self-defense classes before walking back in here.

"Jamison Ferguson, I was expecting you." She disappears again into the back room.

I glance around the store. Newborn clothes hang on small hangers on a display rack. I pick up one and take in how small it is. Guilt chips away at my newfound joy of being in Palmer's life, burrowing deeper and deeper because I missed Palmer when she was that size. What kind of man am I?

"Your order was called in. We only have one available," Mrs. Bennington says, carrying a box out of the back and setting it on the counter.

I pull out my wallet on the way to the register. "I'm glad I got the last one."

She taps the register, never looking at me. "Two thousand five hundred dollars."

I cough. "Excuse me?"

"What didn't you get?" Her fingers tuck strands of red hair behind her ear.

"That's the price of a breast pump?"

I want to say I have two hands that could pump her breasts and she'd enjoy it a lot more, but that's not something Mrs. Bennington would appreciate—or Sedona, for that matter—so I keep that thought to myself.

"It's hospital grade. I talked with Dori about the other ones." She points behind me and I squint to see prices ranging from $65 to $300. "But Sedona is pumping as a favor to Holly and Austin, so this would make the most sense for a single mother of an eighteen-month-old."

Without commenting, I pull out my credit card and hand it over.

She smiles and slides it through her machine. "Dori thought you would agree."

"Uh-huh."

She tears off the paper and I scribble my signature before handing it back to her.

"It's been a pleasure. If she has any questions, please tell her to give me a call. I'm a lactation nurse as well."

I nod. "That's great. Thanks."

"See you soon."

I wave and mumble another thank you.

Once I'm back on the street, I decide to walk to Sedona's instead of hoping to find a spot on Main Street in front of her apartment. It doesn't take long, and when I arrive, I press the buzzer. She immediately lets me in without even a question. That needs to change.

Walking up the stairs with the breast pump in hand, a

million questions swarm my mind. What was it like for Sedona? When did she realize Palmer was deaf? How did she feel when she found out? How did she manage the last eighteen months without the help of a partner?

I knock on the door. After a minute or so, she opens it, wearing a tight camisole that has wet spots over her breasts.

"Jamie!" she yelps, grabbing the edges of her robe and covering herself. "What are you doing here?"

I hold up the bag. "I was sent on a mission to get you a new breast pump."

"Grandma Dori was supposed to bring it over."

Palmer peeks over the couch as if she just realized someone is here. Then she runs and I pick her up in a swoop. She draws back. *Play, Daddy?*

I've never loved a sign more than I do the one for daddy. I shift her to one arm. *Yes.*

"Um, no." Sedona's robe slips open as she takes the bag from my hands so I can hold Palmer easier.

"Why not? You have a situation to deal with. Unless you need my help in that department." I raise an eyebrow.

She shakes her head, but a smile plays on her lips. "Only because I'm desperate, but I'm going to have a conversation with my grandma about this." She turns and mumbles something about Dori interfering as she shuffles over to what I assume is her bedroom.

I shut the apartment door and flick the lock before carrying Palmer back to where she was playing with big Lego-looking blocks. She hands me a yellow one and I stack it on to what she's already started building. She leaves me and goes to a bin, pulling out a baby doll. *Toys.*

I stand to get a better look. She has everything she'd ever need, more toys than a preschool could use. I'll have to get her a gift at some point. Maybe a stuffed animal. Let her pick it out. Something that reminds her of me so she can keep it with her when I'm not here.

Just that thought feels as if there's a binding around my heart that someone is pulling tight.

She rounds the small table and slides her hand in mine, pulling me. I follow her into the second bedroom. It's all girl, her name written above her crib. More toys and stuffed animals fill the corners of the room. A changing table rests along one wall with a stack of diapers on it. Her closet is open, and there are a myriad of cute dresses hung up. She guides me to a rocking chair in the corner, grabs a book, and crawls into my lap. I've never had to do this before.

She flips open the book and touches what should feel like chicken feathers. *Fluffy*.

How on Earth does she know how to sign the world fluffy? We go through the book with her signing *smooth, soft, silk*. She's so smart, I want to wrap her in a bear hug and claim her as mine. But I can't take credit for her.

She lays the back of her head on my shoulder and her hands slide on top of mine, her body heavy in my arms. Then she moves her fingers over my hands and up my arms, where she finds my watch and adjusts my wrist so she can see better. She's a curious girl. A small sigh falls out of her, then her arms lower until they lay limp on mine.

Sedona comes to the door in a pair of yoga pants and an oversized sweatshirt. Her hair is pulled up in a messy bun and she's holding two bags. "She fell asleep, huh?"

I nod.

"Give me one second and we'll move her to her crib. Hopefully, she doesn't leak through."

She disappears before I can ask her what she means about leaking through. My gaze moves to the changing table. Damn it. I should've changed her diaper. I should've known it was her nap time and changed her diaper before reading a book. Any other father would know these things.

Sedona comes back into the room and cringes. "I can't pick her up. All you have to do is stand and lay her in the crib."

"Okay." I do what she instructed. "How have you been dealing with her since yesterday?"

"Well…" She motions with her head to leave the room.

We both leave the room, and she shuts the door behind us.

"How did she get out of the crib this morning?"

Sedona shoots me a sheepish look. "I kind of showed her how to climb out. It's going to bite me in the ass later."

"Sedona, why wouldn't you ask someone for help? You can't do this on your own. Let me help you."

She shakes her head. "You can't stay here. All my siblings have their own lives, and I can't expect Grandma Dori to lift Palmer. She's getting too heavy for her. It's fine. We'll manage."

I blow out a breath, wanting to argue but feeling as though it's not my place.

"I can call you when she wakes up. Maybe you can take her to the park or something." She stands between the family room and the door.

I sit on the couch. "I think I'll just stay. That way I can get her out of the crib for you."

"I said I was fine."

"Yeah, but I think I should stay." I lean back and rest my ankle on my knee.

"Seriously?" Her forehead creases.

I nod and snatch the remote off the table.

She rushes over—as fast as she can, at least—and grabs it out of my hand. "You do not get control of my television."

I hold up my hands. Good thing we're in agreement that I'll be staying put. Now I have to convince her to let me spend the night.

She sits down gingerly in the chair next to me. The television is on and we watch it for a moment in silence.

"Can I ask you something?" I break the ice because I know Sedona—she'll let us skate around the topics we need to address forever if I let her. It's how she keeps her armor up, how she convinces herself to believe things that are happening aren't.

"What?"

"When did you find out about Palmer being deaf?"

Her gaze meets mine and the fearful glint in them alarms me.

"Um... well..." The remote slips from her hand and the next thing I know, her head falls into her hands and she sobs.

FOURTEEN

Jamison

"Sedona." I lean forward, teetering on the edge of the couch, not sure whether I should comfort her or not.

She waves me off.

"I'm sorry. Don't answer if you don't want to. It doesn't matter, right? I mean, we're here, she's deaf, we move forward. I didn't mean to make you upset."

"It came up during her newborn hearing test, but I didn't receive confirmation until months later." She picks up her head and wipes the tears. "I don't really want to talk about what it was like right after she was born."

"Okay, then don't."

I turn back toward the television. I know Sedona—she'll tell me when she's ready. I'm not sure what could possibly have her so upset. She's done amazing with Palmer. But she's yet to trust me, so we'll give it some more time.

As I'm concentrating on a show I don't really give a shit about, I feel her eyes boring a hole through the side of my head.

It's time I share with her what happened after she left me.

"The day you left me, I drank so much I blacked out," I blurt out.

"Jamison, no. It's none of my business."

"I want you to know."

She blows out a breath and nods for me to continue.

"Johnny called and said we should go out, but I said no. I sat on our couch and stared at the ultrasound picture you left me. I convinced myself I was no good for her or you. That I'd fuck up your life more than I already had. With my injury and knowing I couldn't play anymore, I felt as though I had no value to offer. I couldn't give you the life I'd promised."

"All I ever wanted was you," she says in a small voice.

I believe her. Now. But then was a different story. My career had crumbled, and I had no idea what my life would look like after that. And she was pregnant.

"At the time, all I saw was my failed career. Which is wrong. I should've mourned that and moved on, saw my real future with you and Palmer. I'd do about anything to take that back. But I went home and got back in with a few of my buddies who'd taken the college route. Instead of nightclubs in New York City, I was at pubs getting wasted, barely able to see straight. Then I had the car accident."

She nods but looks at her hands. "I saw it on television. It happened right after Palmer was born." A look crosses her face, and I can't decipher if it's one of disappointment or sadness.

I push both hands through my hair, anxiety squeezing my chest like a vise. I should've been with her, not in that car, flipping it off the road and almost killing myself. "Someone saved me that night. I should be dead."

"But you're not."

I shake my head. "No, I was lucky. The worst part is that it took a judge for me to get my arse in line. A fine and twelve months without my license in Scotland."

"And that's when you went into rehab?"

"Yeah. I flew to a treatment center in Minnesota that was highly recommended and continued treatment in Chicago for four months after that. Then it was just a matter of staying clean."

"And your mom and dad? What do they say about all this?"

My heart lurches into my throat. She'll never understand my reasons for keeping Palmer a secret. Just as I think we might find a way to move forward, she's going to slam closed the cage around her heart, I just know it.

"They're happy I'm clean, but there's something you should know."

She tilts her head toward me, and it reveals her usual look of kindness. Talk about twins being opposites. Since the first time I met Sedona, she was so sweet, endearing, and kindhearted. I didn't think I was worthy during those hard days in rehab, wondering how she was carrying on with our baby all on her own.

"They don't know about Palmer," I admit.

She nods and purses her lips, not seeming surprised in the least. "I figured."

"How so?"

"Because if your mom knew that I was pregnant with your baby, she'd be on the first plane out of Scotland. At the very least she would've called me."

She's right. When I tell my mum, I'm pretty sure I should book her an airline ticket immediately. At the time, I didn't want to admit to my parents that I'd walked out on my family because it was just another thing I'd failed at. Her boy, who she was so proud of that she'd brag to anyone in my small town who would listen, had already been stupid enough to risk his entire career by coming back from an injury too early and ruined his future. Then he couldn't handle the pain and drank to numb it, losing the best thing in his life. It didn't exactly put me up for a son of the year award.

"I just couldn't do it… disappoint my mum like that."

If Sedona is upset, she doesn't show it. But she and Mum didn't always get along, so maybe she's relishing this news. It's the same ol' story of a perfect son with a girl Mum didn't think was good enough.

"What's she going to do when she finds out your daughter is eighteen months old?"

"Disown me," I say, gripping my dark hair in my fist.

"Oh, she'll forgive her sweet little boy." She smiles, and all the running jokes between us about me being precious in Mum's eyes run through my brain.

I shake my head.

"Palmer will calm some of her ire, I'm sure."

"Definitely. She's amazing, Sedona."

"Tha—" She stops herself.

I should be on fallen knee, telling her over and over how much I appreciate her doing the heavy lifting for the last eighteen months. Promising her that if she'll allow me, I'll take over the family duties and let her rest. But we're still far from that point.

"I'm so sorry." The words tumble out on their own.

"You need to stop saying that. I know you are, but it changes nothing. I can't be with you again." Sedona braces her hands on either side of the chair and rises slowly as though every inch of her hurts.

She disappears into the kitchen. It's not like we can have a conversation between rooms, so I rise from the couch and join her. She's pulling out a bag of her favorite potato chips from the cabinet.

"I am though, and just because I say it doesn't mean I'm asking for a second chance."

She chomps down on a chip and raises her eyebrows.

"Well yeah, I'd do about anything to win you over, but I'm saying it because I honestly am sorry. If I could turn back time..." I shake my head, listening to Merrick's words in my head about how we can't go back and right our wrongs. We have to own them. "I fucked up my life. But I'm here now to help you. All I ask is for you to give me the chance."

Her head is already shaking.

"Not us," I add. "I mean, I want there to be an us, but if that's off the table, I can't change your mind. Palmer needs a dad, and I plan on stepping up to fill that role. Either we do this together or separate, but I'm going to be part of her life."

Her shoulders fall, and she stares at me as though she wishes a train would come and run me over.

As though Palmer wants a say in our conversation, we hear a bang in her room.

Sedona drops the chips and heads toward Palmer's room. I end up in front of her and open the door to find Palmer smiling and banging her hands on the edge of the crib.

I turn and ask Sedona, "May I get her?"

"Isn't that the whole reason you're still here?"

I disregard her sneer and pick up Palmer. She pats my cheeks with both hands, and I smile. She's so beautiful. Then I realize my forearm is getting wetter the longer I hold her.

I look at Sedona and she laughs. "Well, Daddy, time for a diaper change and change of clothes. Plus, her sheets have to be washed now. Still ready to tackle this daddy role head-on?"

Her eyes hold the same challenge they did when we were seventeen and she dared me to skinny dip in the pond on the Bailey property. Just like I dove in buck naked that day without hesitation, I'm tackling this new role with the same enthusiasm.

She steps into the room and pats the changing table. "Lay her down here." I follow her directions. "Just strip her down to her diaper. We'll have to clean everything."

It's like disrobing a tiger. Palmer doesn't make it easy on me. Not that I can complain when she's smiling.

"I think she likes us together," I say to Sedona.

She blows out a breath, turning toward the dresser. "She's always happy after her nap. That's the whole point of putting her down for one."

"This happy?" I tickle Palmer's stomach and her mouth falls open and she giggles.

"Yep." She sets a new set of clothes next to the table. "Grab a diaper from there and lay it right in front of her open legs. Now take off the old one and put the new one under."

I do as she says.

"Now use the wipes to clean her up—always front to back, never back to front." Palmer isn't having it, so Sedona grabs Palmer's ankles and holds them up. "Like this."

"How on Earth do you have enough hands?"

She giggles but stops abruptly. "I've done it enough times to be an expert."

I nod, concentrating on wiping. Palmer squirms from the coldness of the wipe. "Sorry, baby girl."

"Now pull the sides up and fasten each one."

I do, but the diaper is way too loose. Sedona reaches over me to pull the tabs off and refasten them tighter. I inhale her scent when she leans in front of me. Although she doesn't smell like I remember. Her scent is a different scent now, but it arouses me all the same.

"There you go." She turns before she's all the way standing up.

Our eyes lock with our faces inches apart, and I swallow the lump in my mouth. This is the closest I've been to her since she left me. I'd do anything to break the distance, press my lips to hers and discover if she tastes different now.

She clears her throat and rears back. "Now the clothes. Just like dressing yourself. I'm sure you've got this. I'll prepare a snack for her." She walks gingerly out of the room.

Palmer raises her hand. *Daddy.*

My heart lurches, because I might have told Sedona I was here for Palmer—and I am, no matter what—but I'd give up everything I own to have one more shot with Sedona.

FIFTEEN

Sedona

I don't stop until I reach the kitchen. My hand covers my racing heart while I gather my nerves together. My body was urging me to feel him, touch him, kiss him. To feel with certainty that he's really here and asking for a second chance. How many nights did I pray that he'd return to me?

He smells so good. Not like me, who just gave birth and whose boobs are already busting at the seams to pump again. These hormones must be playing tricks on me. There's no way I could actually still want the man who essentially abandoned me while I was pregnant.

I pull out some cheese and grapes, fixing a plate for Palmer.

Hearing the story of what spurred him to go into therapy made me feel guilty. Should I have tried harder to help him while we were still together? In the months leading up to the breakup, I tried getting rid of the alcohol, asked friends to talk to him. I felt like I did everything I could, and in the end, I didn't want our daughter to be raised in that environment. Still, as I pull the box of crackers from the shelf, my mind travels back to the day I finally had enough.

THE APARTMENT DOOR opens while I'm shoving my makeup bag into my suitcase. Unease settles into my stomach and my phone dings.

Phoenix: *The plane is at the airport. Follow the instructions I gave you.*
Me: *(thumbs up emoji)*

I hear Jamison run into something and mumble a curse word. He never came home last night. It isn't the first time. And if I were staying, I'm sure it wouldn't be the last. He ends up at Johnny's way too often. At first, I thought being around his buddies from the team would help him, but all he does over there is drink even more.

After zipping up my suitcase, I walk out of our bedroom. The one we just redid into something gender-neutral. I stop in the hallway outside the second bedroom. The crib box rests in the corner, unfinished, the sample paint squares side by side on the wall. Leaving my suitcase at the doorway, I step in and take the small New York Storm jersey Jamison bought the night I told him I was pregnant.

I waited a month and told him right before a game. He was thrilled because he said his plan was all coming together. He was back from his injury and starting in the game that night, and now he was going to be a father. He promised me dinner, just the two of us, and a night of lovemaking to celebrate. But we spent that night in the emergency room. Him *getting MRIs and hearing the worst news possible when it came to his career.*

I fold and stuff the small jersey into the front of my suitcase, needing the memory that at one point in our life, he loved our baby.

The wheels on my suitcase slide along the floor, and Jamison's feet hang off the couch while a soccer game plays on the television. It's always one soccer game after another, as if he's torturing himself for not being on that field.

I place the latest ultrasound picture on the kitchen table. Peeking over the couch, his eyes are closed and his clothes are wrinkled and stained. Where did that boy I fell in love with disappear to? Tears puddle in my eyes, watching his chest rise and fall. I haven't seen a genuine smile on his beautiful face in months.

"I'll never stop loving you," I murmur, reaching to touch him one final time.

But I pull back because if I wake him, I'll cower. I'll stay, and I can't do that to our daughter. She deserves more than this. So instead I step back, one step at a time, until I'm at the door. Inhaling a final breath, I soak in the apartment that holds so many good memories—having sex on every surface, the celebrations of games won, coming home to him in the kitchen trying to make my favorite dishes, me seducing him while he watched game tapes for hours.

There are dark memories here too though—the nights spent pacing when he didn't answer his phone, the fights about his drinking, the broken bottle I threw against the wall, the untrusting version of myself who searched his phone for any evidence that he was cheating on me. But I push those memories aside because that isn't us. That's not Jamison and me. We had years of happiness before we had all those months.

I walk out, shutting the door quietly. Outside the door, my feet stop as if they're stuck in tar. My hand runs down my belly. Is it right to take her away from him? Maybe I'm a horrible person. Then by the elevator, I spot an empty bottle of whiskey with a piece of paper beside it. Crouching, I pick up the bottle. It's Jamison's favorite brand, and the piece of paper has a name and number in a girly scrawl.

I drop the bottle, press the down button, and when the elevator arrives, I don't look back.

I'm making the right decision. I just have to make peace with it.

TWO LITTLE ARMS wrap around my legs and squeeze. I glance down to see Palmer all changed and grinning. Jamison is right—she's happier when he's here. Like some wish she's been dreaming of was granted.

I touch her back, impatient to be able to pick her up and hold her close. Taking her plate, I sign for her to come to the table and place the plate down in her spot, then I bend to pick her up.

"Whoa, I'll do that." Jamison swoops up Palmer and places her in her high chair. He figures out the buckles without any help from me.

He pretends to steal a cracker from her, and she claps with a huge smile. Dread fills my body. She's going to prefer him over me soon.

A knock lands on the apartment door, and I don't think I've ever been more thankful to have an interruption. I open the door and Calista walks in with Dion, the two of them beelining it to Palmer's chair and sidling up next to her. Rome follows with an upset Phoebe in his arms.

"Where's Linus?" I ask, wondering what's under the foil-covered dish in Rome's hand.

"A mommy and me class or something. Harley's worried about not getting enough time with Linus." He heads to the kitchen.

Phoebe slides into a chair and mopes.

"Hence the reason Phoebe looks like her hamster got flushed down the toilet. She wanted to go with them," he adds.

"I wanted to go to the park," she says, crossing her arms and huffing.

Rome rolls his eyes. He hasn't acknowledged Jamison's presence yet, but he hasn't cussed him out either, so baby steps.

Calista signs *hi, how are you?* to Palmer. She's just learning some sign language, but I love that she's trying. Everyone has gotten on board.

"Did I tell you that Harley signed up Dion and Calista for sign language classes? Maverick is going too."

"That's awesome," I say, suppressing the urge to cry. Just the thought of how supportive my family has been, brings tears to my eyes.

"You can sign really fast," Calista says to Jamison.

He must have been signing something to Palmer. My attention moves to the table and off Rome.

"I probably started learning around your age. Maybe younger," Jamison says, signing everything he's saying.

Palmer stares at her father as if he's her idol. Rome pokes my side and shakes his head, reading my thoughts.

"I have a great idea! How about Jamison takes everyone to the park?" Rome claps his hands.

Jamison's eyes widen. "Umm..."

"You'll need to bond with the kids anyway. Plus, Calista

will show you the way." Rome slides out the chair Phoebe is in.

"Are you sure? All of them?" Jamison keeps looking at me, and I stifle a laugh.

"Calista is responsible," Rome says.

Palmer kicks the high chair to get out, seeing that everyone is leaving. Dion unhooks her and he tries to lift her out, but Jamison helps. Rome and I work as a team to shuffle them all out of the apartment with promises of being right behind them.

As we shut the door, I laugh and clench my stomach because laughter makes it ache. "You're cruel."

Rome chuckles and puts the foil-covered dish in the fridge. "I put the instructions on top for you. Mac and cheese."

"Thanks." I clean up Palmer's dish and head to the kitchen sink.

Rome washes his hands and leans against the counter, drying his hands with a towel. "Why don't you sit down and take it easy? You're doing too much."

Even though my abdomen aches, I wave him off. "I'm fine."

"Seems like Jamison really wants to be involved. I'm jealous of his signing abilities."

I glance over my shoulder. Rome bears that look. The one that says he drove them out to have a chat. Rome's a great secret-keeper, the only one in our family really. I trust him, but I'm not ready yet to open up. "Yeah, he says he wants another chance."

"With you?"

"Palmer." I take the towel and dry my hands, leaning against the opposite counter.

Rome raises his eyebrows. "Only Palmer?"

"I'm not available."

He nods and looks around. "You got some fuck buddy I don't know about?"

"No. I'm not available to Jamison."

A smirk tilts his lips. "You've been available to Jamison forever. Can I offer some advice?"

"No."

He chuckles. "It's hard to bond with your daughter when you've already missed so much."

"It's hardly the same thing, Rome." If he thinks he's going to compare his scenario to mine, I'll list the million reasons they're different. The first one being that Harley couldn't find Rome. Jamison knew where I was the whole time.

"Different circumstances, sure, but you find yourself in the same situation, right? I mean, here we have a little girl who just discovered she has a daddy. Maybe you should talk to Harley, or maybe it's not the same for you, but she struggled when I started to become close to Calista. She feared I'd take her away. I could've been pissed off at Harley for not trying hard enough to find me, but what would be the point of bringing more animosity into an already difficult situation? Instead we got over our shit, and look, we're so damn happy we can't stop having kids."

"You could slow it down a little."

He shrugs, and his emerging big smile makes me narrow my eyes. No way Harley is pregnant again?

He holds up his hands. "All I'm saying is the guy did a shit thing, but damn, we've all done stupid shit. No one is perfect. But he realized his mistakes and is trying to get on a better path."

My lips purse. "He left his daughter."

Rome tilts his head with an expression to say stop being such a martyr. "Technically, you took her from him."

"Hey, you're my brother."

He laughs and holds up his hands again. "Listen, take this advice for what it's worth. You can do this the long way or avoid more pain and heartbreak and do it the short way."

"What?"

"Well, you can try to fight your feelings for Jamison if you want—but we're not stupid, Sedona, you've loved that boy your entire life. You didn't leave him because you stopped loving him. It's still clear every time you look at him. I know he hurt you—badly—and he needs to make amends with you, but he's on a better path now."

I wave my hand to keep the lecture moving.

"All I'm saying is, you can deny your feelings all you want, but I think you're setting yourself up for failure. No one is going to judge you for loving him."

I cock an eyebrow.

He crosses his arms. "If Phoenix has a problem, she can talk to me."

"And King?"

"Kingston is a puppy dog acting like a pit bull. He'll fold. He views Jamison like a brother. We all kind of do."

He's saying what I've always known. Jamison has been in and out of my family for so long that those attachments are still there.

"Trust me. For Palmer's sake, allow him in. You don't have to get back together with him, but you have to forgive him. If you don't, Palmer will likely resent you one day for not liking her daddy. She'll feel it—if she doesn't see it through body language and the way you two talk to one another." He's silent a moment. "You know, it's funny. When I came back from Europe, I was a little jealous of you and Jamison. You guys had this friendship and respect for one another, along with your relationship. And you were only seventeen. It's still there. Let him make amends for his bad choices."

I nod, though I'm unsure if I'm capable of doing it, especially with my hormones all out of whack.

"Now let's get to the park. Harley's easygoing, but if she finds out I left three of her kids with a guy who just discovered fatherhood, she might have my balls, and I'm not ready for a vasectomy." He opens the door and waits for me.

I follow and decide Rome is right. I have to stop living in the past and move forward—for Palmer's sake at the very least.

SIXTEEN

Jamison

The rental car place isn't that busy, thank goodness, because I want to get to the fire station before Kingston goes on shift. Of course it has to be his engine company that offers free car seat installation checks. Yesterday was the perfect opportunity for me to switch out this car, but Sedona needed me, and she'll always come first now, after Palmer.

When I walk up to the desk, the man who helped me pick out the Camaro two days ago is helping someone else, so I'm left with the woman who looks as though she'd rather be anywhere but here.

"Excuse me, I need to trade this in." I slide over the keys to the Camaro.

"Is there something wrong?" She doesn't take the keys.

"No, I just need a different car. A minivan." I almost choke on the words. I never thought of myself as a minivan guy, but I always see families using them, so I guess they're best.

She eyes me skeptically. "A minivan?"

"Yes," I say, mustering confidence, as if I'm committed to this.

The guy who helped me a couple of days ago stares in disbelief from the other side of the counter. He was spitting out stats to convince me that the Camaro was the rental I'd want when I was in here the first time. Not sure why he cared so much, but he was a soccer fan and recognized me. Then I got the dreaded question of "where am I playing this year?" I hate that damn question.

"You want to exchange the Camaro for the minivan?" this employee of the month clarifies.

"Yes. Is that a problem?"

She finally swipes the keys off the counter and enters the numbers on the key chain into the computer. "Not at all. I'm just surprised."

I tilt my head. "Surprised?"

She types away at the computer. At first, I think she's going to ignore me altogether, but then she finally speaks. "Most men would never make that swap."

"Well, minivans are safer, right?"

She shrugs. "I'm not the editor for *Consumer Reports*."

Good talk. I rock back on my heels as she processes the transfer.

"Same card?" she asks.

"Yes."

Her printer whirs and she grabs paper with an angry pull. I've obviously caught this lady on a bad day.

She slams the papers on the desk. "Sign here. I don't suppose you gassed up the car?"

"I did. I actually got it with three-quarters of a tank, but I filled it up at the station on the corner before coming in."

She smacks on a fake smile. "Oh, would you like a hero cookie?"

What the hell is this lady's problem?

"Gina," the guy next to her says with censure.

Yes, Gina, how big *is* the stick up your ass?

"Do you need me to show you how to use it?" she deadpans, ignoring her coworker.

"I think I can figure it out." I give her a saccharine smile. "I just need to grab something out of the car."

"Fine. I'll follow you." She walks around the corner, throwing the keys to me.

I don't catch them in time, and they drop to the floor.

"Good thing you never needed your hands," she mumbles and walks out the door.

When I meet her at the car, I ask, "Is there a problem?"

She clicks the Camaro open and gestures with her hand for me to get whatever I want. "No problem."

I grab the car seat box from the passenger seat.

"You have a kid?" she asks. "God help them."

I drop the box to the ground. "What seems to be the problem here?"

"It's stars like you who crush kids' dreams." Her eyes suggest she's planning my death or trying to get me to disintegrate right in front of her. "Your posters used to be all over my kid's walls. The local kid who made it to the MLS. You became his favorite player when he found out you went to Lake Starlight High. Then you go and mess up your opportunity with your little drunk driving stint. I'm not sure when you famous athletes are going to understand how much you're idolized. How kids live and breathe to be you. And you guys just let fame and fortune go to your heads and forget that you're subject to the same consequences as the rest of us."

I let out a long breath. She's not wrong. Though she's so under my skin right now, I very much wish I could argue with her, but I'd prefer just to get the hell out of here.

"I'm sorry for that. I was—" I could tell her my entire story with the hopes she'd understand, but there's no excuse for my actions and more importantly, there's no reason to trust her with my truth. I had a responsibility to fans. It's all on me. "I'm just sorry. I hope he found a better guy to idolize."

She crosses her arms and nods. "The funny thing is if I told him that I met you today, he'd kill me for not getting your autograph. How sick is that? He still thinks of you as the best soccer player."

"Good luck to him." I pick up my box and head to the minivan the guy just pulled around to the front of the building. I wish I had more to say, but I'm a fuckup. What does she expect?

I climb into the minivan and look in the back. How fast life can change. I drive a block before pulling into a vacant parking lot and spend half an hour trying to install the car seat. Another failure in my life. I'm starting to get used to them.

I PARK the minivan in the fire station lot. Thankfully, I don't see Kingston's truck. I walk into the office and follow the signs. A female firefighter comes by and says someone will be right out to help me.

Pulling out my phone, I pull up Buzz Wheel and see a post about me watching Rome's kids yesterday afternoon. He played me yesterday, but I enjoyed watching Palmer play with her cousins. They're all so good with signs, and

Calista asked me question after question about signs she wanted to teach Palmer. About what life will be like for Palmer. I'm not sure why she thought I was the person to ask—other than I can sign faster than any of them, including Sedona. It's crazy how fast it came back to me.

I continue reading the article. Buzz Wheel says I'm doing good and how it's proud of me for stepping up. I must know the person who writes this thing, otherwise how would they have all this information?

"Hey." A guy's voice sounds from behind me, and I pocket my cell phone. I turn to greet the firefighter, but he stops in his tracks. "No fucking way. You're Jamison Ferguson."

I nod at the same time as a black pickup pulls into the lot. *Shit.*

The firefighter laughs and looks from the truck back to me. "You sure you don't want to escape now?"

What the hell ? I thought handling this in Anchorage would be easier, with fewer people who know me.

"I should warn you, I'm Lou, Kingston's buddy. I know all about you." He can't stop smiling and laughing. "I should kick your ass for Sedona, but honestly, Kingston would kill me. He'll want to do it himself."

I blow out a breath, hands on my hips.

Kingston presses on the gas, pulling into a spot, and slams on the brakes. He's out of the truck in seconds flat. "What are you doing here?"

"Car seat check," I say, gesturing to the minivan nearby.

He looks over to his friend. "I'll do it, Lou."

Lou taps his imaginary watch. "Technically, you aren't on shift yet."

"It's for my niece. I'll do the car seat." Kingston opens the back door of the minivan.

"Should I referee?" Lou asks, holding up his hands.

"Get lost," Kingston says, the edge to his voice growing.

Lou does the cross over his chest and puts his hands in prayer pose. "That was for your safety, buddy." He laughs and walks back inside.

Kingston tests the half-ass job I did on the car seat. "Surprisingly, it looks good. You do this?"

I'm not blind. He's adjusting it as he goes to make sure it's done correctly. I'm not sure why he's being nice to me.

He finishes up, climbs out, and shuts the door. "Nice van."

"Thanks."

"Decided the Camaro wasn't the right fit?" Of course he knows I rented a Camaro first. "You went from one extreme to the other."

"Well..." I shrug.

He pushes off the van and pulls his phone out before pocketing it again. "I have fifteen minutes before my shift. I wanted to talk to you."

"Are you gonna take me out back and beat the shit out of me?" I raise my eyebrows. I'd probably let him kick my ass because I deserve it.

"I want to, I really do, but you're making all the right moves. Just answer one question for me."

"What?"

"Why'd you wait so long to come back?"

My shoulders fall. "I was petrified. My sponsor suggested not coming here until I had a handle on my disease. I didn't want to make one step ahead for two steps back. You know?"

"But you didn't even acknowledge her. A letter, flowers, a gift. Hell, money."

His words freeze me in place while I try to wrap my

mind around what he's saying. What exactly has Sedona been telling people? "I gotta go."

"Are you serious?" he says, but I'm already climbing into the driver's seat.

I turn the ignition, then open the window. "Listen, King, I've always thought of you as a brother and a friend. I get what I did pissed you off, and I hope like hell you can forgive me one day. But there are two people I have to make this right with, and right now, I need to talk to Sedona. I hope you understand." I roll up my window and pull out of the parking lot.

My anger only intensifies on the drive to Lake Starlight. Walking up to her apartment door, I try to talk myself down, but I can't stand back and allow her to let people think even less of me than they already do. The truth is bad enough.

I knock on her door, and she opens it dressed in yoga pants and a big sweatshirt.

"Where's Palmer?" I barge in.

"She's with Phoenix and Maverick. They went to get ice cream." She shuts the door. "What is your problem? We need to put some rules in place. You can't just show up here."

I hold up my hand to stop her from talking. "I'm done with being Mr. Nice Guy. I'm sick of the 'forgive me for this and forgive me for that' and talking to every one of your family members like their forgiveness means the world to me."

She says nothing but stands in place.

"All I care about is *you* and *Palmer*. Everyone else is second. But for the love of God, tell me why you wanted to paint me as more of a monster than I actually was? What did you get out of it?"

She scowls. "What are you talking about?"

"I sent you money every damn month. I know it wasn't the same as me being here, but I tried to help in the only way I could at the time. And you let your family believe that wasn't the case. Kingston was just asking me why I never paid a dime for my child? Damn it, Sedona." My fist comes an inch from hitting the wall, but I retract it, controlling my anger. I fall into a chair and my head falls into my hands.

I'm done. I have no more fight left inside me.

SEVENTEEN

Sedona

The last time Jamison was this broken was when the doctor told him he'd probably never play again. I don't know what to do. I take one step forward but stop. I tried to hug him when his career ended, and he pushed me away. Looking back on it now, that was the beginning of the end for us.

"I never thought it was their business. No one even asked." When I got the first check from Jamison, I tore it up and threw it in the trash. By the time the second one came, I realized I'd save it all for Palmer. That if she couldn't have her daddy, she could have his money.

"And you didn't think to volunteer the information? Your family shares every time they take a goddamn piss, but not something that might cast me in a better light? That you keep to yourself?" He stands and walks across the room.

"I was hurt, okay? I didn't want to see you in a good light. I wanted you here. With me." My finger points at the floor and I stomp my foot, then I suppress the cringe since the movement hurt my incision. "I didn't want your damn money! I wanted your arms, your heart, your hugs, your kisses, your love." My voice rises as all the pain from the past rushes back.

"It's all I could do at the time. I wasn't fit to be a father or a boyfriend." He runs his hands through his hair.

"And I came to terms with that, but the money felt like an insult. The first check you sent, I was knee-deep in dirty diapers and my nipples were so sore from breastfeeding, they could have been used as sandpaper. You have any idea how hard it was on me?"

He twirls back around. "No, I don't, because you won't talk to me about it, but yer sure hell-bent on making me pay for it."

All the frustration from months of wanting to hash this out with him comes tumbling out. "You think what happened to you didn't break me too? Do you think I didn't weep for you when the doctor told us your professional soccer career was over? I might've put on a strong front for you, but it broke me as well. I knew what soccer meant to you, but I thought we were strong enough to get through it together. But you just pushed me aside. Do you know how badly that hurt?"

"I handled it the only way I knew how. It stripped me of everything. How was I going to support you? Support our baby? I felt like a fucking failure. Because I'd had control of the situation. Maybe if I'd waited longer to come back or wouldn't have been so aggressive on the pitch. The what-ifs plagued me like a bad nightmare. I was embarrassed. Ashamed. I could barely face you."

"We were a team! We'd always been a team. If you'd have just let me be the one to boost us up, to see us through the bad times—"

"That's not how I was raised. I'm the man. I'm supposed to take care of what's mine, and you and Palmer are mine."

His declaration silences me. I can't lie and say hearing those words from him doesn't make my heart float, but that fact alone gives me pause.

So instead, I say, "Well, this isn't the nineteen fifties. I'm not going to stand around with an apron on at five o'clock, waiting to serve you dinner."

He chuckles and shakes his head. "I'm not saying I expect that. I'm just being honest about what was going through my head. Now I'm back, and every time I think we're moving forward, you push me away. You make sure I know exactly all the things I did wrong." His voice rises again.

"What do you expect me to do? Sing your praises for finally showing up?"

He stares for a moment and I swear his nostrils are flaring. "I didn't expect that you'd keep rubbing it in my face every second. I've been here for a week, and though I didn't think it would be an immediate fix, I thought you'd see me trying and maybe cut me some slack."

"I see you trying, and I'm trying too. I'm trying to let you form a relationship with Palmer, but it's so hard to be around you."

He turns around and waves. "Yeah, yeah, 'cause you hate the sight of me. I get it. You've been clear."

My bravado fails and my shoulders fall. "It's not that I hate you. I'm just so hurt. It's hard to be around you because I'm still attracted to you. I still want you and I want to feel the safety you always offered me, but that idea terrifies me. What if you check out and leave me on my own again? You were my best friend *and* my boyfriend."

He slowly turns around, standing in front of me like a defeated child.

"Don't take me struggling to mean that I don't want you in Palmer's life. I do. I just can't decide if I want you in mine."

"Lass," he says, and I close my eyes. "I want to hold you and promise you that I'll make up for the last eighteen months every day, if you'll have me." He steps closer. "I want to wake up next to you, feel the way you'd slide your nose up and down my jaw while you get more comfortable. I want lazy Sunday mornings where we watch Palmer play and promise to get dressed but never do. I want it all." He takes another step closer.

"When you're with her and she's in your arms, it cuts me open." I swipe a tear from my face. "All the hatred for you runs out because seeing you clean again reminds me of the Jamison I loved. The man who would lie down and die for the ones he loved. When I reflect on the precious way you treated me all those years, I know how great you'll be as a father."

He steps a foot closer. "Then why don't we try to get back there? If it's what we both want?"

Before I realize it, he's in front of me, toe to toe, his hand reaching to brush away my tears. My body yearns for his touch. Just to allow his hands on me one more time. What harm could it do?

"I love you, Sedona. You've always been my girl."

I close my eyes. His hand cradles my cheek, and I press my face into his palm, allowing shivers to wrack my body. His touch feels so good, so comforting. I've wondered for so long whether I'd ever hear those words from him again.

"Let me, and I'll spend a lifetime making this up to you."

My body desperately wants to shove all this under the rug. One thing is for sure—I have to admit my feelings for him. Fighting them so hard is only making me miserable.

I cover his hand with mine, and a small smile lifts his lips. "I won't stand here and lie and say that I don't want you so bad that I'm breaking my own heart with what I'm about to say, but I need time."

"Time?"

I nod. "I need to build trust between us again." He draws back, and I step forward this time, gripping his hand. "I'd bet on you. I know we're going to get there, but I'm not ready. Not yet. You're a great guy. You always were, and now that you've committed to sobriety, you're going to be a great father. I have no doubt about that. I've been so set on putting you in your place after all this time, but I've been hurting myself by doing so. So if we're going to do this, let's do it. But let's start slow—as friends."

"Friends?" His voice cracks as if he can barely stand to say the word.

"We've always been great friends." I grip his hand harder.

He nods reluctantly. "Okay."

"And I promise no more mention of the past. I'll talk to my family."

"Can I hug you?"

I shake my head. "Not yet."

He nods as if he's okay with my decision. "Want to see my new car?"

He drags me by the hand to the window looking down on Main Street.

I open the blinds and look up and down the road. "Which one?"

"The black minivan," he says proudly.

I turn toward him and narrow my eyes. "You went from a Camaro to a minivan? Oh, Jamison, I have been putting too much pressure on you."

Imagining him driving the minivan around like a soccer dad, I laugh. He laughs too, and I end up grabbing my stomach because I'm laughing so hard, I'm afraid that I'm going to rip my stitches out.

"I can't take it back. The woman at the car rental place hates me."

"Why would she hate you?"

"Long story. Maybe I should buy myself a car here."

"You think you're ready for that type of commitment?" I ask. "Maybe you can get one of those big conversion vans next?"

He doesn't laugh, although I can tell he wants to, and for a moment, I'm able to forget everything that happened in the past. Maybe there's hope.

Then the apartment door opens, and Phoenix is standing there scowling at us enjoying one another's company. Palmer sees Jamison and kicks in her stroller to be freed.

"Is that your mom-mobile down there, Ferguson? Nice kiss-ass move."

Jamison says nothing. Maverick, the sweetheart he is, unclips Palmer, who runs straight to her daddy. He picks her up with ease and kisses her cheek.

Phoenix shoots me a look across the room like *you're not really buying his shit, right?*

I watch Jamison and Palmer, and yeah, I'm buying it. Aren't there stages of grief? I think I'm over the angry phase. I want to move forward because I do still love Jamison. It's just the trust we have to work out.

EIGHTEEN

Jamison

I'm close to Sedona's apartment on Main Street with two bags from Hammer Time Hardware when my phone vibrates in my pocket. My phone doesn't blow up like it once did, so it's likely one of two people—Sedona or Merrick. My money is on Merrick since he left me a concerned voicemail yesterday. Concerned meaning he's worried I'm off the wagon since he hasn't heard from me.

Stopping at a bench, I place the bags down and answer his call. "Hey, man, I'm sorry. It's been crazy here."

"So you're good?" His voice is calm and steady, even though I know he's worried. The man's Zen-like state amazes me.

"I am. Things are progressing."

"Really?" He sounds in disbelief. Merrick doesn't know Sedona and has his doubts about whether we could make this work. He didn't know us as a couple and the love that was there.

"Yeah, we're trying to be friends at the moment."

"Okay," he says, concern in his tone. "Well, I wish you luck. Have you been to a meeting?"

I sit down next to my bags. "No."

"Jamie, you have to go to a meeting. You need to find a safe place. We agreed that you'd attend one as soon as you arrived to town. Your life is in flux right now, and it's not the time to skip out on what helps with your recovery."

I nod. "Yeah, I just got distracted."

"I know you're excited to finally be there and back with Sedona and Palmer. I saw how hard you worked to get healthy, but you won't stay that way if you don't keep doing the work. The work is the meetings."

"But—"

"No, I don't want to hear any excuses. Get yourself to a meeting today. I'm glad you and Sedona are finding common ground, but you never know how it's going to turn out. If you don't set yourself up in a good spot, the end of you and Sedona could be the end of you too."

Merrick isn't really a tough love kind of guy. He's more of an encouraging teddy bear. But right now, he's got the same tone my mum used when she got mad at me for my messy room.

"I'll find one."

"Good. Anything else you need to talk about?"

I shake my head even though he can't see me. "I'm good."

"Okay. Call me if you need me."

"I will." Things with Sedona and I are on track and I want to keep it that way, meaning I hope I don't need him.

"Take care of yourself, Jamie."

"I will."

We say goodbye and I hang up, sitting on the park bench for a moment to collect my thoughts. He's right, I know he's right. Merrick has gotten me this far, and just like I would listen to my coach on the pitch, I'm going to listen to him. So I hit the search engine on my phone and find a meeting. Not in Lake Starlight though. Anywhere but Lake Starlight.

WHEN I ARRIVE at Sedona's, Austin, Holly, Easton, and Harper are just leaving.

"How're the new parents doing?" I ask.

Austin switches the carrier to his other hand. "I could use some more sleep but I'm not complaining." He looks down into the carrier with so much love in his eyes it almost feels like I'm a bystander in a private moment.

Holly rolls her eyes. "Last I checked, you weren't getting up for the midnight feedings." She chuckles.

"Hey, that's only because I have to get up for work."

"Mommy, I'll do a feeding for you if you want," Easton says.

We all chuckle and Holly musses with his hair. "Thanks, buddy. You're a great brother."

"She's a beautiful little lass. Congrats again." I nod and squeeze past them, not an easy feat with all these bags in my hand.

"Bye Jamison," Holly says before leading Easton down the stairs.

Austin turns and faces me. "How are you doing since you arrived? Good?"

I can tell by the way he's asking what he really wants to know is whether I'm back on the sauce.

"I'm doing well. Nothing to worry about there."

He nods and leaves the way Holly did.

I knock on the door and Sedona answers a few seconds later. "What's in the bags?" she asks.

"I'll show you. First, let me say hello to my girl." I set the bags by the front door and close it.

After I've played with Palmer, I decide to get to work while Sedona fixes a snack for Palmer.

"Jamison, you don't have to do this." Sedona places some cheese and crackers on Palmer's tray while I install a new strobe light that will go off when someone rings Sedona's doorbell. "She can't answer the door on her own yet anyway."

I turn around, thankful my dad made me help him with small projects around the house when I was younger. "I know, but it will get her used to it for when she's older."

She tears open another box that arrived on her doorstep and sighs. I think she's a little annoyed at the things I've purchased. "She has books, Jamie. I'm not a horrible mom."

Palmer watches me intently while she eats. She's quiet today, and I like the way I'm starting to understand her different moods. She's not cranky, but Sedona said Palmer woke up during the night a few times, so she's tired.

"I know yer not a horrible mum. These are just things I found when I was researching. Which reminds me, I wanted to ask you about something."

It was hard for me not to go ahead and call Sedona the minute I read an article about cochlear implants. But it was two in the morning and she's still healing from her C-section.

"I can only imagine." She waits for me to go on, thumbing through some of the books with her feet up on another chair.

"I read that some kids can have cochlear implants to help them with their hearing?"

She nods. So she knows what I'm talking about. Her lack of excitement says either we're going to have a tough conversation about whether to try them or not, or she's already been down this route.

"I talked with her ENT doctor when she was eight months old. She's not a candidate." A small frown mars her face.

"Really?" I try to push back my disappointment. I had such high hopes that she'd be able to hear even minimally one day.

She nods. "Sorry."

I pretend to steal a cracker and Palmer snatches it back from me before I can pop it into my mouth. She giggles and I kiss her cheek.

"Why would you apologize?" I ask Sedona after I'm back to installing the light.

"I can see that you were excited. Like maybe she could overcome her deafness."

The tone in her voice makes me stop what I'm doing. "True, I'm disappointed, but it doesn't change anything."

"She's perfect." But there's a chip on Sedona's shoulder that wasn't there a moment ago.

Okay yeah, I think she's misunderstood me. I hold up my hand. "She is. I never said she wasn't."

"Then why ask about a cochlear implant? Even if she were a candidate, do you really understand what it would mean for her? The teasing? The medical complications? How she might be viewed by the deaf community? Trust me, the deaf community is small enough in this area. I don't want her to be ostracized from them. My support group is online because we're almost all too far from one another to have in-person meetings and I have to travel to Anchorage to see her specialist." She picks up the signs I bought for the lights and some other stuff. "And all this stuff? The new light, the books, the sign language mat for her room? Do you think I'm not doing what I should for her?" She stands slowly from the chair, gripping her stomach, and disappears into the kitchen.

"This has nothing to do with what you're doing. She's amazing, and I'm well aware that's all because of you. All of this is just to help her. The research—"

She huffs. "Do you think I didn't do my own research? I was the one sitting through the doctor appointments and—"

I break the distance, cornering her against the counter. She draws her face back so we're not as close. "Breathe. This isn't me making up for some lack of parenting on your part. This is me trying to be a parent. Finding stuff that I hope will help her. I don't want her to change, but you bet your arse I want her to have every advantage life has to offer. I'm trying to be a real partner to you, not your competition."

Her shoulders fall, and I take her hands in mine. "Sorry. I may have overreacted."

"It's just the Phoenix side of your personality coming out."

She shakes her head, but a smile tips the corners of her mouth.

"Yer an amazing mother. I'm trying to help her, that's all. And you. I mean, if you've never spent a dime of the money I sent you, how have you gotten along this entire time?"

Last I knew, she was freelancing for different online magazines, but when I was with her, it wasn't paying all the bills. Then again, I took care of the mortgage on our condo and all the bills.

"Nothing you need to worry about. But there is something I have to talk to you about." She nudges me back.

I reluctantly break away from her. "What's up?"

We go back to the small kitchen table area and find Palmer asleep in her chair. Her head lazily slides to the side and pops back up, then back down again.

"She's exhausted," she says.

"Can I put her down?"

"Sure."

I unstrap Palmer, and she transfers into my arms perfectly.

"Don't forget to change her," Sedona says.

I nod, wondering when I won't get the reminders anymore, but given how long my daughter was without me, I haven't been back for long. I need to give this time.

I change Palmer's diaper, get her settled, and lay her down in her crib.

When I return to the living room, Sedona has the screwdriver in hand, finishing the job of installing the light.

"Excuse me," I say and hold out my open palm for the screwdriver.

Sedona laughs and hands it over. "I was just trying to help you."

"This is that manly thing where I like to prove myself, remember?"

She holds up both of her hands. "Sure thing. Have at it. I wanted to ask you something." She sits on the chair nearest me.

"What's up?"

"I have my appointment at the doctor's tomorrow for my two-week follow-up. I'll be clear to drive afterward, but is there any way you can drive me there?"

"Sure. Definitely." My answer is quick and decisive.

"Around nine? I'm going to ask Kingston to watch

Palmer."

"Can she not go?" I ask.

"It's easier without her truthfully."

I sit on the chair next to her. "What if we took her and then went somewhere after? Like the park, the zoo, somewhere just the three of us?"

Our gazes lock, and I can tell she's working through it in her head. I brace myself for the no.

She shrugs. "Sure."

"Really?"

"Yeah. I think Palmer will really like that."

"I'll be here at eight-thirty?"

"Perfect."

For the rest of Palmer's naptime, I continue doing some odd jobs while Sedona cleans the kitchen. Other than a few sly glances where I caught her looking at me because I was checking her out, it's a platonic afternoon. I have to think if she weren't fresh off a C-section and we were in a different place, we'd have spent the downtime in bed together.

That night, after I leave Sedona's, I find a meeting in Sunrise Bay. I sit down in the circle of chairs in the church basement, and when it's my turn, I stand and announce my new truth that still rattles me with the fear that I could very well end up there again.

"Hi, I'm Jamison, and I'm an alcoholic."

"Hi, Jamison," the small group says in unison.

I sit back down and drink my water.

Merrick was right. The most depressing part of my day is when I leave Sedona and Palmer to spend a lonely night in my room at Glacier Point. I could easily slip out of control if I'm not careful. I'm not sure how I'd handle it if things don't work out between us, and I don't want to end up looking at the bottom of an empty bottle of booze again.

NINETEEN

Sedona

After strapping Palmer into her car seat, we climb into Jamison's minivan rental.

"I feel like I should take a picture to preserve this fine moment." I hold up my phone.

"You do and I'll take one of you when you leak," he teases.

I shove my phone back into my purse. Unfortunately, Jamison has seen me leak through too many times. I'm not used to nursing without a baby around, and I'm not on a good schedule with my pumping. I push myself too long most days.

As he drives, I give him the directions to my doctor's office. I watch him maneuver the minivan around town and still can't get over how odd it looks. A minivan just doesn't fit Jamison.

In the parking lot, he takes care of Palmer, even carrying the diaper bag. Seems weird not to be wheeling a stroller and having my hands full of stuff while I get us from point A to point B. A girl could get used to this.

Once we're in the doctor's office, we sit, and Palmer goes to play with another girl and some toys in the corner. We watch her share blocks, then the girl asks Palmer her name and she doesn't respond. The mom glances at us and buries her head in her magazine. The little girl dips her head to Palmer and asks again, telling her her name and that she's three.

When Palmer still doesn't respond, the little girl approaches us. "Can she talk?"

Jamison stiffens next to me, and I place my hand on his. "She's deaf."

I rise to get up, but Jamison's hand slides out of mine before he gestures for me to sit. He crouches down to Palmer's level, getting her attention. He signs to her the girl's name and that she wants to know Palmer's name. Palmer smiles at the little girl, then signs her name as though the little girl should understand her.

"Her name is Palmer," I say. "She just used sign language to answer your question."

The mom peeks up again and closes the magazine, leaning forward to touch her daughter's arm.

Palmer looks at the little girl and smiles again. *Hi. Nice to meet you.*

The little girl asks how old she is. Jamison sits cross-legged and acts as an interpreter between the two, signing the entire time even though Palmer probably won't catch all that he's signing.

The mom looks at Jamison as if she wants to eat him up, and protectiveness runs hot in my veins.

"Sedona Bailey," the nurse calls.

Jamison signs to Palmer to say bye, which she does.

"You can stay here if you want. It might be a little... graphic," I say.

Jamison continues to stand, picking up Palmer. "No, I want to hear what the doctor says."

"Um, why?"

"Because you won't be truthful with me about your restrictions." He winks at me and smiles at the nurse. "This is Sedona."

Katie, the nurse's eyes shoot up to her eyebrows. "I'm aware. And who are you?"

"Katie, this is Jamison."

"I'm Palmer's dad," he says proudly, and my heart skips a beat. He passes Katie and walks down the hallway.

"Exam room four," Katie says and follows him with her gaze then looks back at me. "Oh. Nice," she whispers.

I smile and follow her to the exam room. Inside, Jamison is already on the guest chair with Palmer, bouncing her on his knee as if she's on a roller coaster. Her body wobbles around. Though Palmer's always been a happy baby, with Jamison, her smile is a little wider, a little fuller. She's already fallen for him.

Dr. Estes knocks and peeks her head in. She eyes Jamison, then me. "Hello."

"Hi, Dr. Estes, this is Jamison Ferguson—Palmer's dad." I almost choke out the words, but they do come.

She smiles and puts her hand out for Jamison. They shake hands, and she signs to Palmer. *Hello. How are you?*

Hi. Palmer points at Jamison with a big smile. *Daddy.*

Dr. Estes looks at me and grins. Yep, everyone thinks this is great. Palmer's happy, Jamison is happy, and I desperately want to be happy.

Jamison sets Palmer so her legs are on either side of his thighs and he raises his hands. As Dr. Estes asks me questions, Jamison signs most of what we're saying. I'm sure Palmer has no idea what he's signing. He's superfast.

"I don't think you have to do that?" I say as Dr. Estes pulls up my shirt to look at my incision. "And turn around." I point at him.

He rolls his eyes but does concentrate his vision on Palmer. "If she could hear, she'd hear every word. I know she can't catch up on what I'm signing, but she'll learn the same as a child who can hear." Jamison signs what he's saying to me.

"That makes perfect sense," Dr. Estes says, and I want to ask her whose side she's on. Does she not remember the crying mess I was, coming in here eight months pregnant with Palmer? Traitor.

"And she's a doctor." Jamison waggles his eyebrows.

I blow out an annoyed breath. "His ego is big enough, Dr. Estes."

She smiles at me and checks my incision. "Everything looks good. You can drive now, but I still need you to be careful as far as stairs go and too much lifting. No exercising until I see you at six weeks." She sanitizes her hands and goes over to her computer. "Pain level okay?"

Sitting up, I allow my feet to dangle off the bed. "It's good. How long until I can laugh and it won't hurt?"

She smiles as though she understands. "You'll get there. I know it can be hard. Especially with this adorable girl."

She tickles Palmer, who looks at Jamison. He signs and she giggles, but I think it's only because Dr. Estes tickled her. What do I know? Maybe Jamison is right. I've been working on my sign language, but I'm not nearly as fluent as Jamison is. Which means I better study more. She already looks at him as though he's her hero.

When we leave the doctor's office, Palmer gets a

lollipop from the office girls who keep looking at Jamison and pointing out how much Palmer looks like him. I breathe easier once we're on our way to the minivan.

"You always have a fan club no matter where you go," I say with a slight sneer in my tone.

"I'm surprised they didn't crucify me. Was she your doctor with Palmer?"

I nod, my lips pursing. "Yep."

He straps Palmer in the car seat. "They forgave me. How long for you to join them?" I stare blankly, and he laughs. "I'm kidding."

"You're not."

He double-checks the fasteners on her buckles. "Yer right, I'm not." He shuts the back door, then climbs into the front with me. "I'd like nothing more than for you to forgive me so we can move on." He turns the key in the ignition.

"I'd love if my mind just magically agreed with my heart."

He nods, but I don't think he really understands why I haven't forgiven him yet. I'm not even sure I do. My body hums every time he's near.

"Let's just enjoy today. I shouldn't have said anything." He pulls out of the parking lot and we head to the zoo. "Do you think yer up for it?"

"Yeah, I can handle the walking. Just don't laugh at me if I sit every chance I get." Palmer will want to look at the animals, so I'll have plenty of time to rest.

"Not a problem." I can tell he's excited to take Palmer to see the animals. It's kind of sweet.

In the zoo lot, we climb out and he takes out the stroller, again taking care of getting Palmer out of her car seat. I grab the diaper bag, but he snatches it away and places it in the storage part of the stroller. He pays for us to get in, and we enter the zoo like a real family. The thought makes me melancholy.

Palmer kicks the foot of the stroller when she spots the polar bears.

"Those are her favorite," I say to Jamison, so he heads over there.

After unstrapping her, he holds her as she giggles and claps when one of the bears hops off a rock and into the water. I sit down on a bench, a little sore, watching their backs. My heart aches from having him so near and being unable to touch him, unable to let him in.

Jamison lowers her and signs to her all about the polar bears, reading facts off the information plaque. She laughs, when he puffs up his cheeks with air after he's told her how much the polar bears weigh, and she slaps his cheeks. Then he pretends to loom over her with both arms and she ducks under, running over to me.

I hold her to my legs, but she climbs them, and Jamison continues acting like a bear while breaking the distance to us. Palmer curls up in my chest as though she's really frightened, and Jamison bends over, nestling his face against her neck as if he's going to bite her. His scent reaches me and my entire body zings with awareness. He's so close.

She squirms, and I'm so lost in his nearness that I don't notice when she crawls down while his arms remain on either side of my head. We're face to face, inches apart. Years ago, he would've kissed me, and I would have thought nothing of it except wanting him to do it again.

Today, tension fills that small gap between us like a grenade with the pin half pulled. I want to fist his T-shirt and drag him to me, smash my lips to his, and never come up for air. He bends forward, reading my body language like the pro he is when it comes to me. I put my hand over his lips.

"Not yet," I say in a quiet voice.

He nods and stands straight, then he picks up Palmer and makes her fly as though I didn't just crush his hope like his eyes suggested. I don't know how much longer I can hold out.

We walk through the zoo, Palmer in Jamison's arms the majority of the time. He buys us pretzels, slushies, and all the junk food we could want. At the gift shop, Palmer walks out with a giant polar bear that drags on the ground. We put him in the stroller, and Jamison holds a sleepy Palmer to his chest.

"Thank you," I say when we get settled in the van. "It was a nice day."

"I had so much fun." The way he looks at me, with so much hope and admiration, makes me suck in a breath.

We drive to my apartment and I allow him to help me bathe Palmer and put her to bed. After we shut the door of her bedroom, I feel close to collapsing, but I stand by the kitchen table to say goodbye.

"Can I ask a question?" His tone is serious.

I stiffen. "Sure."

"I want to tell my mum about Palmer. I feel horrible for not doing it yet and spending the day with her made me realize how much I've stolen from my mum already."

"I never wanted you to keep it a secret."

He nods. "I know, but you know mum. She's going to contact you, she's going to want to visit, and we're just getting on the same wavelength. I don't want to set us back."

"It's fine, Jamison. Things are changing, but this is good. The more people who love her, the happier she'll be. Go ahead and tell your mom."

He wraps his arms around me, and I'm quickly trying to find my axis again. His scent, his strong arms, his breath in my ear—it takes me on a dizzy ride where I lose sight of my goal—protecting my heart.

"Thank you," he says in my ear, almost breathless.

His palms run up and down my back. I close my eyes at the feeling I've missed most since leaving him. He steps back and runs a hand through his hair.

"Sorry," he mumbles, glancing at me through his dark eyelashes.

Oh, who am I kidding? In this moment, there's no part of me that wants to resist. I step forward and throw my arms around his neck, smashing my lips to his. He doesn't miss a beat, wrapping his arms around the small of my back, locking me in place. His tongue slides into my mouth and he groans, spurring my arousal.

It's been so long, and this feels so good. Damn, I want to climb him, straddle him, feel how hard he is. The lack of sex and orgasms over the last two years made me needy.

The doorbell rings and the light he installed flickers into strobe mode, and I strip my lips off of his. He steps forward, his hand on my cheek. I point at the light, and he sighs.

"Forget it," he says, hooking his finger in the waistband of my yoga pants to tug me toward him.

"Open the door, Sedona!" Phoenix is on the other side.

My head falls to his hard chest.

"I know you're in there. The man van is outside."

I look at him as he gets that defeated look on his face. "I should go anyway."

I don't stop him because I think the kiss probably came too soon. It was like adding wood to a raging fire, and one day, no one will be able to douse the flames.

TWENTY

Jamison

It's been three weeks since I kissed Sedona. We spend the majority of our time together. I'll watch Palmer sometimes while she's trying to write a piece. Today I convinced her to join me on a picnic by the lake. I kick the soccer ball to Palmer, and she tries to kick it back but misses and ends up on her butt.

I run over, but she stands back up all on her own. Way to go, little lass.

"She's only nineteen months," Sedona says from the blanket where the food is spread. She pops a grape into her mouth.

"If I start her now, she'll be the youngest to ever play in the World Cup."

Sedona shakes her head. "I meant to ask you about your plans. It's been over a month now."

"I'm not sure exactly what yer asking." I pass the ball back to Palmer, but she gets distracted and chases a butterfly, so I head to the blanket.

"You mentioned the coaching thing once but haven't said anything else about it."

I nod. "Yeah, I don't see that happening. I doubt yer going anywhere, and Palmer is so happy here." Since I arrived, I haven't truly thought about a job. I've been preoccupied with getting Sedona back and having the three of us be a family. I'm fortunate that I haven't blown through all my money from when I was playing professionally, but it won't last forever. I pick at a blade of grass. "I have to figure something out though. My bank account is taking a hit from Glacier Point."

Her silence makes me wary.

"Are you trying to get rid of me?"

"No," she rushes out and my heart eases a little. "I just wondered if you were leaving."

I glance at her, but her eyes remain on Palmer. "I told you I'm not going anywhere without you."

She nods but doesn't look at me.

"Sedona," I say.

She glances at me for the briefest second but doesn't let her vision stray from Palmer for long. "What?"

"I don't want to rush you, but when do you think you'll forgive me and give me a second chance?"

"We'll talk about this later. Right now, our daughter is about to go for a swim." She stands, but my gaze flashes to Palmer, who's at the water's edge.

Adrenaline shoots through my veins, my heart pounding in my ears as I sprint as fast as I can and grab the back of her shirt right before she could fall into the water. She cries, and when Sedona gets closer, Palmer holds her arms out for her. I wrap my arm around Sedona's waist and kiss Palmer's head.

"I've never been so scared," I say.

She closes her eyes and holds our daughter tightly. "Welcome to parenthood."

I hold them both close, never wanting to let go. We hug for a few moments until a familiar voice interrupts us.

"Be careful, you'll be in Buzz Wheel again," Kingston says.

We turn, and Sedona steps away from me. Buzz Wheel is so fucking annoying. The last time we were in it was the day we spent together at the zoo. Turns out some Lake Starlighter snapped pictures of us to report to the gossip site. Hence the reason Phoenix showed up and ruined our kiss.

"Hey, King," Sedona says.

Palmer perks up when she spots Kingston, and Sedona lowers her to the ground. She runs to her uncle with arms wide open. I shouldn't feel jealous. My little girl has so much love to give.

He crouches down and hugs her. *Hi, how are you?* Then he picks up the soccer ball and twirls it on his finger.

"It's not a basketball," I say.

He snickers. "I was teaching her to throw a baseball." He pretends to do that damn *Karate Kid* movie stunt where Ralph Macchio bounces the ball from knee to knee.

I break the distance and steal the soccer ball mid-flight. "Let a professional do that."

Kingston smiles and nods. "Hey, I'm not the wedge anymore. I've made my peace with you." He holds up his hands.

Palmer sits on the blanket and grabs a cracker, watching me interact with her uncle.

"She's happy, I'm happy. Which reminds me. I wanted to talk to you, Jamie." He looks at Sedona. "Alone."

"Um, okay... why?" she asks.

As if Kingston planned it, which he just might have, Grandma Dori walks down the path with Ethel at her side. "Oh, what a beautiful family setup. Right, Ethel?"

"Love the picnic." Ethel sits on a nearby bench.

Dori comes right into the middle of us, waving to Palmer, who gets up and hugs her great-grandma then goes over to Ethel and hugs her too.

"We're going to take Sedona and Palmer to Clip and Dish," Dori says.

Sedona shakes her head. "Um, no. We're good."

"They're expecting you. I know having a baby is hard work." She touches Sedona's hair. "Your hair has lost all its shine, and these ends…"

Kingston covers his mouth to keep from laughing out loud. Sedona hits him in the stomach. He buckles over, and I laugh.

"She's beautiful," I say.

"Kiss ass," Kingston coughs out.

I shake my head. If I could, I'd nail him in the stomach too.

"Don't be jealous that I got all the good looks in our family." Sedona strolls past him, throwing her hair over her shoulder.

It's nice to see her carefree personality returning.

"Anyway, let's go get pretty," Dori says to Palmer.

Palmer looks over her shoulder at me. *What?*

All eyes zero in on me. I sign to Palmer what Dori said. I think she just understands go and pretty, but she takes Dori's hand.

"What is this?" Dori asks Jamison.

"Jamison signs all our conversations now. Regardless if it's age-appropriate or not." Sedona tucks her chin down and looks at me from under her lashes.

"Not dirty talk, I hope?" Ethel chimes in from her perch on the bench.

Sedona shakes her head. "There is no dirty talk happening in our household."

"Yet," I say.

Sedona's cheeks turn a bright red. "Can you handle cleanup?"

I pick up her purse from the blanket. "Yeah, go and enjoy your time."

Dori winks at me. Kingston and I watch the three women and a baby head toward Main Street. They disappear around the corner and my phone dings a few seconds later as I'm cleaning up the picnic.

It's another unknown number, but it's the same one as last time.

Unknown Number: *Be at Sedona's at five-thirty. Dress in a suit.*

I shake my head.

Kingston tries to look over my shoulder at the screen. "What's going on?"

I close the lid on the grapes and stuff the container into the basket of food I surprised Sedona with. "Nothing."

"Seems like you have a matchmaker on your hands and it's not Juno." He holds the basket while I fold the blanket.

"Why are you being so nice to me?"

"Because I haven't heard from Sedona in two whole weeks. Which means you must be doing your job as a father. Plus, Sedona told our group chat to stop acting like you have to make amends to us. You only have to kiss her ass, which I see you're doing a damn good job of."

"Thanks?"

He clasps his hand on my shoulder. "It's my sister and my niece. I had to protect them."

I nod. "Well, it's my job now."

"Yeah it is," he says. We head toward my minivan, Kingston already laughing before I click the key fob for the sliding doors to open. "Seriously, man, you gotta trade this thing in."

"It's a family mobile. I'm a father." Truth is, the woman at the rental shop scares me. I don't want to listen to her lecture on why I'm a horrible person again.

"A father of one. You're not Rome. He's gonna have to purchase a bus soon."

We both laugh. I always loved Kingston. He's only a couple years older and we always got along. He'd be the one who messaged me on game days with a "great goal" text. Something to let me know he was watching.

I change the subject before I head too far down memory lane. "You said there was something you wanted to talk to me about?"

We drop everything in the minivan. "Yep, I have a business opportunity for you… well… us." I cock an eyebrow, and he chuckles. "It's a good one, don't worry. Let's go for a walk."

And we do. We walk around the lake while Kingston tells me his business plan. But the hook is, he's not looking for an investor. He wants an actual partner.

TWENTY-ONE

Sedona

Clip and Dish isn't too busy, which sadly leaves no excuse for them not to do my hair. Most of Grandma Dori's friends come here and it's her hairdresser who's going to do my hair, so I'm worried.

"Don't worry, hun, she's good with modern hairdos too," Ethel says and bounces her silver locks in her palm as though her hair is "modern." Maybe Ethel doesn't realize that perms aren't all the rage anymore.

"And she's a great colorist," Grandma Dori adds as if her blue-tinted hair would be an endorsement.

"I think I can just get a trim," I say, examining the ends of my long dark hair.

I have kind of let myself go. Then again, I don't live off of Jamison's money, which I did when we lived together. And working behind a computer every day, you don't have to pretty yourself up. Palmer doesn't judge me if I stay in my pajamas with a messy bun in my hair all day. It's sort of a writer's uniform. But for the first time in a long time, I want to change that.

Marie comes out of the back and claps when she sees me. "Dori said her granddaughter was coming in. She talks about all of you so much, but none of you ever come in to see me." She pretends to pout, and I glance at Grandma with questioning eyes.

She shoos me, and I follow Marie toward the back. I point at Palmer before I go. "Don't let anything happen to her."

"Ethel could use the practice. She doesn't have any great-grandchildren yet."

I walk backward, Grandma following me, and watch as Ethel allows Palmer to stack nail polish bottles on the table. Marie leads me to the wash sink.

"Just a trim, Marie. You can just wet my hair if that's easier."

"Nonsense. Dori said a shampoo, a bikini wax, the entire works."

"Wax?" *Oh, God no.*

"Yes, dear, it's been a while." Grandma leans over the sink to look down at me. "You need to look good down there."

I cross my legs. "Can we not talk about waxing?"

"We're all ladies. There's nothing to be ashamed of. Your grandfather—"

I hold up my hand. "Please stop. Please."

I never knew my grandfather—he passed before I was born—but I swear Grandma thinks we want to know all about their entire relationship, including the bedroom.

"Fine, but if he liked it, maybe Jamison does too. You're missing out." She sits in the chair at the sink next to me.

"I was with Jamison for long enough to know what he likes." *Why am I even entertaining this conversation?*

"It's been a long time. His tastes could have changed."

"Marie, isn't there a rule about only having customers in the back?" I look up at her as her long nails dig into my scalp. It feels like heaven and sends shivers down my neck.

"Oh, sweetie, I think you know that no rules apply to your grandma," she says.

Grandma Dori pats my knee. "See? She's sweet, unlike my ungrateful grandchildren."

"Can you at least check on Palmer?"

The door chime rings, and Dori perks up next to me. "No need! There are our reinforcements."

A million little voices ring out and I hear Harley telling everyone to quiet down.

I bolt up and soap runs down into my eye. "You called Harley?"

She pats my knee. "Sit down. And yes, I did. Palmer loves her cousins."

"Harley has enough on her plate."

Marie gently pushes me back over the sink with a hand on my shoulder.

"Oh, you have it all wrong. She's going to give you a massage. Denver is coming too. Kingston's going to meet him, and they'll take the kids to the park until you're all relaxed."

Harley comes back and pats my leg. "Hey, girl, I hear tonight's the lucky night."

"What are you talking about? I came here for a haircut." I shift to get up, but Marie shoves me back down in the chair again.

"Almost done," Marie says.

I peek up with one eye to see Harley above me. "You're in on this?"

"I thought you were in the know. Dori?"

"Please, none of you would get anything done without me." Grandma Dori stands and walks toward the reception area. "Grandma Dori has candy!"

All the kids scream, and I hear Calista telling Palmer to come with her.

"Don't worry, Palmer is following. Calista signed to her." I can hear the pride in Harley's voice. "Jamison has had quite an effect on her. I caught her watching a YouTube video the other day about signing."

I glance over and Harley's smiling proudly. She's a great mother.

"While you get a cut, since this was all a surprise, I'm going to drive them to the—" she stops. "Never mind. I hear Denver."

"What's up, munchkins? Your favorite uncle is here," Denver says, and all the kids cheer.

"And don't worry, Stella's going to the park after she's done working. A doctor is good to have around with this lot." Harley touches my knee.

I feel oddly vulnerable and exposed.

"Dori gave them candy, so unless you're hiding ice cream, you're nothing right now," Harley yells toward the front of the shop.

"Is that the lucky lady?" Denver's voice grows closer. "You want Cleo to call you with some tips? I know it's been a while."

I hold up my hand. "Okay, enough with all this. No one said anything about me getting lucky."

I stand with the towel on my head, and Marie guides me to her chair.

Denver plops down in the chair next to me. "From the way I heard it, you could've gotten lucky weeks ago." Denver holds up his hand to stop himself from talking. "Oh, but you were preggo. That's right. Damn you for being such a great sister."

"First of all, it hasn't been six weeks yet, and second—"

"Didn't you have a C-section?" Harley asks, sitting on my other side.

"Yes."

"So technically you could do it at four weeks, if your doctor gave you the go-ahead."

"Seriously, only you would know the guidelines of when you can have sex after birth. You're probably knocked up again." Denver twirls around in the chair.

"Please don't do that," Marie says.

Denver stops, which for him is progress.

"Let's get back to the topic at hand. So are you getting back together with Jamie boy or not?" Denver asks.

"Of course she is," Harley says. "From everything I've seen and heard, they're meant to be together."

The door chimes again. Damn it. What now? I look through the reflection of the mirror, but I can't see the doorway.

"No worries, all. Jamison has no idea what's happening tonight." Kingston walks in and takes the seat next to Harley, twirling it around. Marie says nothing to him about it, but then again, he smiles with those two dimples that always let him get away with everything. "Hey, Marie, love the new color."

Harley and I stare slack-jawed while he flirts with a sixty-year-old woman.

I finally yell above the chaos, "Can someone please tell me what the hell is going on and why I'm not in the know?"

The salon quiets except for the sound of Calista rounding up the little ones for a round of Duck, Duck, Goose in the middle of the salon.

"You're going on a date with Jamison tonight," Harley says.

"No, I'm not."

Everyone's chairs twirl toward Grandma Dori, who says, "I make no apologies. He'll be at your door at five-thirty. And please don't fight this. I've seen you since he returned. He's made amends, and it's best to get on with it. We all had a vote on it."

I look right and left without moving my head while Marie quietly clips my hair, probably logging all this for an email she'll send into Buzz Wheel later.

"Seriously?" I say to them all.

Harley holds up her hands. "I thought you knew. Honest."

"I think you've made him suffer with blue balls long enough." Denver holds up his hand. "I voted for the date."

Kingston says nothing but tries to lure Palmer to him, probably using her as a distraction.

"And you, King?" I ask.

He shrugs when Palmer is more interested in playing with her cousins. "I always liked Jamison, and he seems like he's doing well. I want you to be happy and I think Jamison makes you happy, so I voted... yes."

"Sorry, Rome must have voted yes," Harley whispers, then mumbles something about not being asked.

"This is a good thing. I have no idea why you're acting like you don't want him," Denver says.

"I saw you guys hugging at the lake." Kingston cringes.

"Yes, because Palmer almost fell in the lake. Jamison caught her."

"Rome and I bonded over Calista that time she cut herself," Harley says. "Sometimes you have to share that fear to realize no two people love your kid as much as you guys." She smiles. "But if you think you're not ready, then don't do it."

"Harley, can I speak to you for a moment?" Grandma Dori asks.

Harley's eyes roll and she stands.

"Oh, you're in trouble," Denver teases.

Marie shoots Denver a look to say get out of my shop.

"Why is everyone up in my business?" I ask.

Kingston slides over to where Harley was sitting. "Um... did you not grow up as a Bailey?" He twirls again in the chair.

I'm not sure any of us have grown up over the years.

Denver leans forward as Marie pushes my head so my chin touches my chest. "Honestly, are we not supposed to be on Team Scotland?"

His eyes make it clear this is a genuine question. I sigh. My body is weakening toward Jamison, and yes, Dr. Estes told me because I had a C-section, I don't have to wait any longer if I feel ready. But it's a big step.

"Oh please, we're totally Team Scotland," Kingston says. "You know you love him. He fucked up. Big time. But it's not like he did it because he's an asshole. He was tackling an addiction, and as far as I know, he's clean and sober now. Why torment the guy any longer?" Kingston shakes my leg.

They're lucky Phoenix is in Los Angeles right now. I'm sure she'd be up for explaining to them all why they're wrong.

"Please stop touching her," Marie says, lifting the scissors.

"Sorry, Marie." Kingston smiles at her.

They're right. It's not like I'm against it anymore. It's just been figuring out when the time is right. Every night when he leaves, I yearn for him to stay and share my bed with me, but I chicken out and don't say anything.

"Let Stella and me take Palmer for the night," Kingston offers.

"How come he always gets her? I'm her uncle too." Denver swivels. Palmer is looking toward us, so he pats his leg. "Come here, Palmer."

She shakes her head and grabs Calista's hand.

"Man, I swear I'm the better-looking brother." Denver sounds perplexed as to why his niece wouldn't stop what she's doing and race over to him.

Harley raises her hand. "Rome's definitely the best-looking Bailey brother."

Denver's eyes narrow. "We're identical twins, Harley. How do you figure?"

"I guess personality can make you more attractive." She laughs.

Denver jumps up from the chair. Harley rushes away from him and puts Dion in front of her. Dion gets on the defense and puts up both hands as though he's going to protect his mom. We all laugh, including Denver, who takes Dion from Harley and puts him over his shoulder.

"Sorry," I mumble to Marie.

"It's fine." She smiles, looking through the mirror at the chaos behind her. "You're all done. I'll blow you out, then we'll go do the wax."

"That's not necessary."

"It's not just about the man's pleasure. It will make you feel beautiful too." Marie pats my shoulders and steps away to grab some product to put in my hair.

She's right—I need to feel beautiful. I look through the reflection of the mirror at my crazy family here for me. They'll catch me if this goes south. Why keep myself from something I want just because of fear? He did make a mistake, a huge one, but it was a mistake just the same.

First things first though—I have to tell him about right after Palmer was born. He deserves to know I'm not so perfect either.

TWENTY-TWO

Jamison

At five-thirty sharp, I show up at Sedona's door wearing a suit I bought from Mr. Johnson. Which reminds me, I have to figure out what to do with my condo and the rest of my stuff in New York.

I ring the bell and wait. Sedona opens the door, her dark hair cascading down in long spirals, her makeup done perfectly, and wearing a dress that covers everything but makes my hands itching to touch her.

"Hey," she says.

"You look gorgeous." I might as well be that pathetic dog with his eyes popped out of his head and his tongue hanging out. Sedona's always beautiful whether she's hungover or she's dressed for a night out, but I haven't seen her like this in a while.

"Thanks. I wish..." She shakes her head. "Are you ready?" Leaving me at the door, she swipes her purse from the small table by the door.

"Where's Palmer?" I ask as she locks up her apartment.

"She's with Kingston and Stella tonight."

Although I miss seeing my little girl, having a night out with just Sedona more than makes up for it. "They're all very hands-on with her. They don't treat her deafness as something negative or leave out because of it, huh?"

She side-eyes me as we walk down her stairs to the street below. "They've all been really good about including her. They do their best to communicate with her, but I hope she learns to read lips as she gets older. It will make life easier for her. I understand now why you're always signing as you're talking to her. That will help. I need to do that more."

I open the building door that leads to the street and she slides by me. "It's hard to remember to do it."

I can't give her parenting advice. She's been at it for almost two years, and I'm still a newbie.

When I reach out to touch the small of her back, I retract my hand because we're not a couple anymore. She glances at me as though she has the same thoughts. God, it's excruciating being so close to her physically but so far emotionally.

"Your chariot awaits."

"It's a minivan." She quirks her eyebrow.

I nod. "There's a lot of room in the back should the mood arise."

She smiles and says nothing, sliding into the passenger seat. It has to be a good sign that she didn't take the opportunity to shut me down.

Once we're settled in the car, my gaze strays to her shapely legs. Her legs are the part of her I love the most. When I came home late from traveling back from a game and her leg was peeking out from under the sheets, no matter how tired I was, I craved her. My vision skates along her body and I relish the memory of her underneath me.

Our eyes lock and she fidgets as though she's remembering the same thing.

"I'm not the same," she says.

Sedona and I always did communicate well without words. One look and we knew what the other was thinking.

"Yeah, you are." I start the van and pull away from the curb.

She's quiet for a moment. "Pregnancy changes your body. Now I have a C-section scar adding to what Palmer already did."

We stop at a red light before I have to turn onto the interstate toward Sunrise Bay. "I don't care about any of that."

"I just thought you should know in case the time comes—"

"When," I clarify.

She giggles into her hand. Once again, no hand in the air telling me no. Another good sign.

"Well, don't expect to see the same woman. There are stretch marks and I'm not nearly as thin." Her hands press to her stomach and she inhales a deep breath.

I cover her hands with one of mine. "I'm positive it's as beautiful as always."

A soft smile lands on her lips, but I'm not sure she believes me. In a way, I understand where she's coming from. I've seen my body change now that I'm not working out with trainers and running across the pitch nonstop. But I wish she could see herself through my eyes.

"I'm not the cut guy you used to drool over."

She huffs. "Drool? Me?" She points at herself.

The light turns green, so I turn onto the interstate. "Come on. You loved my body as much as I love yours."

When I came back from Scotland to play in the MLS, her gaze ate me up all the time she saw me without a shirt. I wasn't blind. I never minded her ogling my body, but I have the same insecurities she has. I'm still fit and muscular, but my abs aren't nearly as well-defined as they once were. My days of ten percent body fat are gone.

"Maybe, but drooling is kind of an exaggeration."

I glance toward her, and she turns to look out the window.

"So we're both insecure about our bodies... are we thinking lights off tonight?"

Another huff as if she's annoyed by my forwardness, but not actually putting me in my place. "You're way too much tonight."

She likes it though. She always used to like it when I talked like that. Of course it used to be a lot dirtier, but I don't want to push her too far.

Getting off the interstate, I drive into Sunrise Bay and pull in where the GPS on my phone tells me to. It's the parking lot of a bed-and-breakfast.

"You know I didn't make this reservation, right?" Parking the minivan, I pull out my phone to double-check, and yeah, it's the same address the mystery number texted me.

"I know, I wasn't exactly turning you down, but this is a big assumption," she says from the passenger seat, staring at the inn sign the same way I am.

I scan the area because I have to be missing something. Sure enough, there's a small restaurant attached to the north side of the building. I point. "There. A restaurant."

I exit the van and walk around to open up her door. We

walk across the parking lot to the door for the restaurant called Seafins. Inside, the space has huge windows that showcase the glittering bay and the mountains visible in the distance.

"It's gorgeous." Sedona's hand falls on her heart. "How did I never know this was here?"

"I have no idea." I'm just as speechless from the view, and that's saying something when you've spent so much time in Alaska.

The hostess comes over with a wide smile that makes me think she knows who we are before I even give her my name. Grabbing two leather-bound menus, she walks us to a table right beside the window. We thank her and sit, barely able to take our eyes off the view.

A waiter greets us before we have a chance to look at the menu. "Welcome to Seafins. Can I get you anything to drink?"

Both the waiter and I defer to Sedona.

"A glass of..." Her eyes meet mine with a guilty look. "Just a Diet Coke."

"She'll have a glass of pinot noir," I correct because it's always been her drink of choice at a fancy restaurant. She gets pinot noir, and I'd get whiskey on ice.

"No. I haven't had caffeine in so long. I want the Diet Coke."

I stare at her long and hard, but she doesn't budge. Blowing out a breath, I look at the waiter, who surely doesn't understand our push and pull. "I'll have a Diet Coke as well."

The waiter walks away, and Sedona busies herself with taking her silverware out of the cloth napkin and laying it over her lap.

"Sedona?"

She peeks up at me and shakes her head.

"You know you can order whatever you want."

"No. I'm not doing that. I'm not going to sit here and drink in front of you." She leans back and crosses her legs under the table.

"You can. I'm good. I've been around people drinking since rehab. I'm not going to—"

She puts up her hand. "Jamison, I love you, I always have, and I'm not going to sit here and enjoy something that might be tempting for you. It'd be like if I were on a diet and you decided to sit in front of me and eat a chocolate cake."

I chuckle. "I think you mean if I was eating a carton of ice cream."

"True. A carton of cookies 'n cream ice cream."

"Honestly though, I'm good with you drinking. If we're going to move forward, which I hope we are, you can't just refuse to drink when I'm around. That's no life for you. Yer not the one with the problem. I am."

"You can't force me to drink."

The waiter interrupts us, placing the sodas on the table. "Do you know what you'd like to eat?"

"Can we have a minute?" I ask.

The waiter nods and heads over to the other tables he's responsible for.

Sedona picks up the menu. "What looks good? I think I'm going to have the tilapia."

"I'm not gonna drop this. This is a thorn in the side for us moving forward, and I'd really like to remove it." I put down my menu, but she keeps reading hers.

"You have to pick two sides. Want to share?" She tips her menu down. "I mean, is that weird since we're not really a couple—" I steal her menu. "Jamison!" she whisper-shouts.

"We're not going to ignore this issue. We can't."

Her shoulders sink. "Can we please just order?"

This isn't the Sedona I know. She doesn't ignore a problem, hoping it will go away on its own. She's the type who organizes and cleans her junk drawer until every item has a spot.

"We can't until we talk this over."

"I get it, okay? But I don't see what the big deal is that I want to support you and not drink." She crosses her arms.

"I appreciate it, and that's not what I'm saying. It's the fact you don't want to talk about it."

She leans forward. "What exactly is *it*?"

"My addiction. My alcoholism."

She tears her gaze from mine and chews on the inside of her lip. The waiter starts to approach, but I put up my hand, and he circles back around to the bar area.

"It's not easy, okay? It's the one thing you chose over me," she says.

"It was never a choice."

She nods a few times as though that makes sense. "But it felt like it. Like you chose alcohol over us."

A tear slips down her cheek. Fuck me. How did I not see this?

I hold my open palm out for her hand. She glances at it and her hand slowly meets mine. I run my thumb over her knuckles. "My addiction had a power over me that it doesn't anymore. I'd never willingly pick anything over you and Palmer. You have to believe me."

She uses her other hand to wipe her tears. "I do. I know it's a disease, and you didn't really choose it per se, but I hate it. It's what took you away from me."

"Believe me, I hate it too, but it's my reality. And suppressing my feelings and not trying to work out problems is what got me there in the first place. Now when something comes up, I need to deal with it right away."

Her fingers grip my hand. "I am really proud of you. I don't think I've told you that."

The cracks in my heart that formed when I ruined my life with Sedona fill and heal with her words. "Thank you. But I don't want you to change your life for me."

She sits up straighter. "Don't you see, Jamie? I would stop eating cookies 'n cream ice cream for you. I'd do just about anything to make sure you're happy. And if it means I don't drink wine, I don't really care."

"Just know it's an option. I won't bounce out of the wagon because you had one glass of wine."

She nods. "Okay."

"Have you thought about going to Al Anon? It might help you."

"I tried when I first had Palmer, but I never followed up with it. Maybe I'll try again." She smiles. "So how about we try to have a normal date without carrying the weight of all the baggage?"

I clear my throat, hand her back the menu, and look mine over. "I was going to have the special. Figure the catch of the day has to be fresh."

"I think I'm going to stick with the tilapia. Would you like to share some sides? I promise I don't have cooties." She grins. God, I love seeing that on her face again.

"I'd love nothing more than to get your cooties. You pick."

We finally settle into our dinner, pushing away all our issues so that we can just be Jamison and Sedona again.

TWENTY-THREE

Sedona

My cheeks hurt from laughing through dinner. I forgot how much Jamison made me laugh with his stories.

"And I had to climb the stairs to get on the subway system. I thought they ran underground." He's telling a story about the Chicago transit system.

"There weren't signs?" I quirk an eyebrow.

He guffaws. "Not that I saw." But the tint in his cheeks says he's embarrassed, thinking back on the story.

The waiter interrupts our laughter with a platter with a silver dome cover on it. We glance at one another because we know this isn't the cobbler we ordered to share.

"Grandma Dori?" I say.

"Or her sidekick." He slides it my way. "Want to do the honors?"

I put my hand on the handle. "Not really, but..." I lift the silver dome and inside is a keycard. Picking up the keycard, I find a small note. "And we have a note."

Jamison takes the keycard, reading the name of the bed-and-breakfast that's attached to the restaurant. "This is such a *Bachelor* moment."

I laugh because he hated when I forced him to watch it with me. "I think she's thrown subtlety out the window."

I straighten the note to read it. Sure enough, Grandma had someone write the note for her.

YOU'VE WON one night's stay at the SunBay Inn! A beautiful suite with a view of the famous Sunrise Bay is awaiting the two of you to enjoy. Please see the innkeeper next door, and don't worry, all toiletries are included. Wink wink.

Good for tonight only.

Cannot be redeemed for cash value.

I HAND the note to Jamison and he reads it. "Does the 'wink wink' mean what I think it means?"

"Oh, if I told you what happened to me earlier at Clip and Dish, you wouldn't look so surprised." Just the thought of Grandma Dori talking about waxing—and oh, I can't. Although I understand her persistence now.

"Aren't you still unable to do anything?"

I tilt my head, my smile betraying me. "Is someone keeping track?"

His smoldering eyes lock with mine and he leans forward, lowering his voice. "Once I get the green light from you, I'm not about to stop myself. But I knew we had to wait, so I've mentally prepared myself."

"Lucky for you, the doctor gave me the okay."

"But aren't you still in pain?" He eyes my stomach as if it's a gaping wound.

"Not really. I mean, more the inside, like when I laugh or cough, but I could probably manage. You know, if I really had to."

A smirk crosses his lips. "And do you have to?"

I pick up the note and tap my lips with it. "I'm not sure. I think I'd like to give it a try."

Jamison raises his hand. "Check, please!"

I laugh.

After Jamison pays, we walk out of the restaurant to the inn, where we locate our room listed on the keycard.

"You know there's going to be rose petals and God knows what else in there?" I say as he inserts the card, waiting for the green light.

"All I care about is having you in the room with me. Alone."

Then we're in the room. A silent room. A room with just us and no distraction of Palmer. And it all becomes very real. I'm going to have sex with Jamison Ferguson for what feels like the first time when it's really probably the hundred thousandth time. I feel as if we're two different people.

He deadbolts the door, and I'm thankful we have our own bathroom.

There are no rose petals strewn on the bed, but there is a basket with some snacks, waters, and condoms. I pick up the package. "I guess they took care of everything."

He shrugs out of his suit jacket and tosses it on the armchair. Then he's coming toward me and my throat closes up.

"I come to you in peace." He holds up both hands because I'm sure I look as nervous as I feel. I nod, and his hands take the box of the condoms from my hand. "Dori alone was bad enough, but with Ethel, they could rule the world." He places the condoms on the table. "No pressure, Sedona. I know I've been making cracks, but if yer not ready, then it's fine."

His hands settle on my hips, and all I really want to do is walk into his arms and have him hold me.

"Can we start with a hug?" He opens his arms.

I don't wait a second before stepping into him. His big arms wrap around me like they always did, and I lay my head on his chest. His heartbeat pounds in my ear and I slide my arms around his taut waist.

"I love you," he whispers, kissing the top of my head. "Our time apart has been horrible. You might not believe me, but—"

I draw back and place my finger on his lips. "No more talking about the past."

He nods, and I go back into the position of him holding me. Nothing makes me feel as safe and secure as Jamison's arms. As though no one could harm me. We sway as if we're dancing. He hums a song I haven't heard before, but it's slow and I like it.

"What song is that?" I ask, not breaking our rhythm.

He takes one hand off my back and pulls out his phone, thumbing through something before setting it on the table. Music plays. "It's 'I'm Yours' by The Script. It just makes me think of you. Of us."

I rest my chin on his chest and look up at him. "Ever wonder how we found each other so young?"

He kisses my forehead. "I would never question what brought me to you. I'm just thankful that I found you. I'm only upset about how much time I wasted."

I strip my gaze away from his. "There's something I have to tell you," I murmur into his chest. "Something that might change that look on your face."

He steps away from me, grabs his phone, and lowers the volume. "Come." Taking my hand in his, he leads me to the edge of the bed. "Nothing will take this look off my face. Yer my entire world. You and Palmer."

But he's wrong. What I'm about to tell him could change it, but if we're going to truly start fresh, he needs to know. "Don't say that yet."

"What is it?" He dips down so our eyes meet.

"After Palmer was born, I fell into a bit of a depression. After her diagnosis, I didn't know what to do. How to give her the life she deserved. Whether I could afford her medical costs or even help her. To be her advocate. The doctors said it was postpartum depression. Stella still reminds me that it happens to a lot of women, but I wasted time lying in bed, feeling sorry for myself, while my family helped take care of our daughter."

He closes his eyes.

"I know. I'm sorry. Here I've made you feel horrible about not chasing us and not being there when I had my own secret." Seriously, how hypocritical can I be?

He laughs and puts his finger under my chin for me to look at him. "I love hearing you say *our* daughter. You've never referred to Palmer as our daughter."

She sighs. "Jamie, are you listening to me?" I stand from the edge of the bed. "I allowed others to care for her. I didn't get out of bed. I lost all my baby weight plus more. If it wasn't for Kingston and Stella, who knows what would've happened? I was a mess."

He leans forward with his forearms resting on his legs. "You were a young single mother who'd just found out her baby was deaf. That's a challenge for anybody. I'm not trying to boost my ego, but you were still dealing with the loss of me in your life too."

"That's no excuse. It's a mother's instinct to care for her child and I just left her with other people." I stare at the floor and shake my head. He doesn't understand the severity. I wasn't taking care of our child.

"I will not allow you to feel guilt for what was out of your control. Your hormones were going crazy, not to mention your life had just changed profoundly and then changed again with Palmer's diagnosis. You were bound to crash. Yer not superhuman." He stands and again urges me to look at him. "Didn't we just say the past is the past?"

"I wanted you to know. In case that changes anything."

He puts his hands on my cheeks to make sure I can't tear my vision away. "All it makes me feel is more guilt that I allowed you to live through that alone. But I'm here to tell you that I'm never leaving your side again. End of story, okay?"

I nod, not convinced. But I did forgive myself as much as I could a year ago—after a therapist told me that I can't keep feeling guilty about the past. I have to live with it but forgive myself.

"Can I kiss you now? You don't have anything else to divulge to me?"

I shake my head. "Conscience clear."

"Good." He bends forward, and I rise on my tiptoes to meet him halfway.

Our lips touch and I've never felt so much spark from one connection. It's always been like this with Jamison. I inch closer, unable to be close enough to him, and his hands wrap around my back, molding to my hips until I'm flush against him.

The kiss is hurried, our lips battling for dominance in a game that neither of us wants to lose. But it's been so long. So long since I've been with anyone. My libido is as fast as a

Learjet racing down a runway. I go from nothing to needy in an instant.

"Take off my dress," I say, falling down to my heels and turning around for him to get to the zipper.

He lowers the zipper too slowly for my liking. If he ripped it, I wouldn't be upset. His palms aren't nearly as calloused as I'm used to when they skim across my shoulders, urging the fabric off my skin to pool around my waist. I'm about to push it to the floor when his lips press against my right shoulder blade.

"I've missed you," he whispers. "Your beautiful body. The way your skin breaks out in goose bumps when I touch it. I can't wait to hear the moans that float out of you." His hands push the dress down from my hips and it cascades to the floor. His fingers unhook my bra and he slides it off my body until it joins my dress. "Still so damn beautiful. I've dreamed of this exact moment so many times during the years we've been apart, but none of it lives up to being here now, with you. To have my hands on your body, my lips on your delicate skin."

He clears his throat as though his emotions are getting the best of him. I circle around, and his gaze washes over my body up until it lands on my face again. There's no disappointment or regret. If anything, his eyes only become more ravenous.

"Make love to me, Jamie," I say and wrap my arms around his neck, pressing my mostly naked body to his.

His large hands slide under the elastic of my panties to grab my ass. Turning us around, he eases me down on the bed and I elbow my way up while he disrobes not nearly as fast as I'd like him too.

"Grab the condoms," I say right before he's about to join me on the bed.

"Good thing yer the smart one out of the two of us." He tosses them on the bed, and they land right next to my head.

His lips fall to my skin and my eyes close, reveling in the feeling of being home again. All those fears about the changes in my body disappear. I should've known better. Jamison loves me, not my body.

This man has owned me since the first time I saw him on my high school soccer field. From the first smile. First flirtatious glance. First handhold. The song he played is called "I'm Yours," and that goes both ways for us. I'm his forever, and he's mine.

TWENTY-FOUR

Sedona

Jamison's lips stop at my C-section scar and I inhale a deep breath. He presses his lips to the scar and continues casting small kisses up my torso until his mouth covers my breast. He twirls his tongue around my nipple, making it grow harder. Good thing I stopped pumping two weeks ago, but I'm worried the stimulation might cause me to leak.

Our legs are entwined as he kisses me, his hand on my throat, dictating where he wants me. His tongue runs up my neck, his hard length grinding into my center. I raise my hips to meet his and he chuckles, shaking his head. Then he disappears down my body, nestling himself between my legs. Both hands run along my inner thighs, widening me for him. He lightly kisses my clit and our gazes meet.

"Ride my face?" he asks. Years ago, he would've just flipped me over and urged me above him. "I mean, if yer up for it."

I slide up in the bed. "Stop treating me like a grandma. Lay down, buddy." I point at the bed.

"Bad reference," he says.

I laugh. "I didn't actually say Grandma D—"

He shuts me up with a kiss that erases all memory of what I was saying. He lies down and his arms are bent beside his head as though he's ready. I lay one knee on each side of his head. His hands run up my back and guide me down to his tongue that's already poised and ready to taste me.

He moans the minute I allow my weight to bear down on his face. He hasn't forgotten what makes me tick, his mouth and his tongue working me expertly as his hands slide up my torso and grab hold of my tits. It's all delicious, but the moans and groans floating out of him take me to the brink. Knowing he's enjoying this as much as I am only spurs my own arousal.

I bend backward, grinding into his mouth, and he reacts by moving one hand to the lower part of my stomach, his spread hand keeping me in place.

It's amazing how it's one of those things you never forget. Our rhythm of how we work together to reach the same goal is there after all this time.

Soon, I'm crying out and clenching. He's holding me down to prevent me from rising up because I'm going to explode like a round of fireworks.

"Right there. Oh shit. I'm coming."

My orgasm hits me with a force that almost knocks me down. I was fooling myself when I thought my dildos were on par with this.

Letting me ride it through, Jamison doesn't stop even after my quick jolts from the now-sensitive nerves his tongue is manipulating. I climb off and down him to give him the same pleasure, but his hands plant under my arms and he brings me back up.

"No way I'll survive that tonight. I want to come while I stare into your eyes."

I'm surprised when he puts me on my back. Jamison isn't really a missionary kind of guy. His favorite position is him standing and me lying down on any surface. The kitchen counter was his favorite in our New York condo. But his knee nudges my thighs open and he settles between my legs, sitting back on his ankles.

I watch him pull back his foreskin and roll on the condom. "I guess we'll be careful, huh? Don't want another Palmer." I'm not sure of the reaction my face shows, but he's quick to add, "Yet. Give your body time to heal."

I raise my eyebrows, watching the latex roll down his hard girth. "Do you want another baby?"

He tosses the foil wrapper to the side of the bed and kisses the stretch marks that Palmer started, and Harper worsened. "I want to see your belly swollen with my baby again when I can really appreciate it." He cups my tits, thumbs running over their hard peaks. "I want to hold your hand during birth and cuddle next to you on the bed with the baby." He kisses right between my breasts. "I want to see Palmer as a big sister. I know it's selfish of me, but I missed so much with Palmer. I'd love to experience it all with you."

His declaration makes me want to slap a sold sticker on him, but we're far from ready for any of that.

He crawls up me. The tip of his dick circles my opening without sliding in, teasing me mercilessly. He bends his head and his lips meet mine, our tongues tangling in a dance we perfected at age seventeen.

Just when I'm prepared to beg him, he slides into me.

We both moan in pleasure as he works all the way in with small thrusts. After so long without any action, I've grown tighter and unaccustomed to the feeling.

"Shit, Sedona, you feel fucking amazing."

He plucks the words right out of my head.

His breath labors in my ear as he slowly pulls back then pushes in again. "I'm never going to last to a respectable amount of time. Forgive me now."

He grinds in a circle, taking his time until I run my leg up and around his waist. He lifts up on his elbows, casting the smallest kisses on my face. "I love you so much, lass. Thank you for trusting me again."

I hate that I keep comparing him to before, but this is the Jamison I loved in New York. The sweet boy who hadn't let fame go too much to his head. The boy who loved a girl and never wanted to let her go. We strayed so far from each other, I can't believe how easy it is to come back to the familiarity of one another again.

His movements are gentle, as though he's afraid to break me. It feels amazing, but I don't want him to hold back.

"Harder," I say.

He looks into my eyes. "You love me, right?"

His vulnerability throws me, but I give him an honest answer. "I love you. So much."

His lips crash to mine, and it's as though someone put a stopwatch on us. Our hands claw and grip. Our mouths collide. The pace he sets becomes frantic. We're like animals out in the wild, claiming and overpowering each other.

He slides out of me, moving to the bottom of the bed to stand, and he yanks me down by the ankles, his dick quick to push back in again. With his hands on my hips to keep me in place, he drills into me. "Yer tits jiggling like that are killing me."

I feel them shaking and I grab hold of one, twisting my nipple. His eyes turn hungrier as if he's about to scream "mine" and feast on me. I'd have no complaints if he did.

"Tell me yer close, lass," he says.

I raise my hips off the bed, meeting him thrust for thrust until that familiar tightening begins again. His thumb touches my clit, sending me through the universe like a shooting star. I clench around him and cry out until my body releases all its energy and I lie limp on the bed. Shit, how can the second be more powerful than the first?

Knowing I came always makes him more aggressive. Lifting my ass off the bed, he takes me exactly how he wants, but right before he comes, his hand slides around the back of my neck. He pulls me to him, kissing the heck out of me as he growls, pumping and stilling inside me.

Even after he comes, he keeps me there, resting his forehead on mine while we both try to catch our breath.

"Better than I remember."

"Definitely."

He releases me, and I fall back to the mattress. He disappears into the bathroom and returns, pulling down the covers for us.

I crawl in first. "So you haven't had sex since..."

He smirks and kisses my nose. "Nope. I haven't." He shimmies down the bed. "Now come and let me hold you. I missed the cuddles too."

I do as he says, resting on his chest and enjoying the skin-on-skin feeling. I smack his chest and he looks quizzically at me. "That's your sold sign. You're mine."

He kisses my forehead. "I've been off the market since the first time I saw you."

I raise an eyebrow. "You thought I was Phoenix."

"No, I mean, I did, but after Miles told me and you were waiting by the picnic bench, I saw you, the real you. And I fell in love."

I swat his stomach. "Please, you did not."

He laughs. "Okay, maybe not love at first sight, but it was pretty damn close."

I press my lips to his chest. "Yeah, me too."

It was all such a fairy tale until the glass slipper shattered into a million pieces. It all feels the same again, as if no one can touch us, but I'll never be foolish enough to let my guard down again.

TWENTY-FIVE

Jamison

A knock on the door the next morning wakes me, and I look to my side to find Sedona asleep and facing the other direction. We went through all but one condom last night. I pull off the covers, put on my slacks from last night, and open the door.

A friendly woman with red hair, dressed in a sundress and sandals, beams at me. She holds a large covered basket. It's weird and uncomfortable.

"Hi, I'm Mandi, the owner of the SunBay Inn." She peeks her head in but I step over to obstruct her view. "I brought you guys some breakfast. Nothing too big. You're welcome to come down to breakfast if you'd prefer, but my grandma told me to deliver you something to keep your energy up." She rolls her eyes while trying to remain professional.

"Thank you, Mandi." I take the basket from her. "Who's yer grandma?"

I'm fairly sure Dori doesn't have any more grandkids.

Sedona's dad was an only child. But I guess you never know.

"Ethel Greene. She and..." She moves to peek in the room again. "Sedona, right?" She points toward the bed.

I nod.

"Sedona's Grandma Dori cooked up this whole thing. I do apologize. Usually I'm not one to help with my grandma's crazy schemes and I'm sure you guys don't remember me, but our schools played one another back in the day. You were Lake Starlight's soccer star. After everything..."

Seriously? She's not going to remind me of all this now, is she?

"Anyway, I have a soft spot for a true love story and couldn't resist helping them. I do hope you enjoyed your stay, and no worries, you're on the late checkout list." She smiles brightly and waves goodbye.

"Life is never dull with Dori around," I mumble, shutting the door.

Sedona is awake and sitting up. She's slipped on my dress shirt and is buttoning it.

"Hey now, no one said you could get dressed." I put the basket of goodies on the bed and curl up next to her, nuzzling her neck.

"Who was that?"

I blow out a breath. "Yer never going to believe who owns this inn—Ethel's granddaughter, Mandi. She's our age and I guess she loves a good love story, so she helped them out." I open up the basket. "No complaints here though."

"Me either." She sits closer to examine the basket. "This is so cute."

There are muffins, jams, fruit shapes on skewers, cups of granola—anything anyone would want for a continental breakfast. I take a blueberry muffin, unwrap it, and hold it up to her mouth. She takes a bite, then I do.

"It's so good." Sedona snatches the rest of it from me.

I stare at her and she looks at me like *what*.

"Guess we're over that whole first date thing?" I chuckle.

She rolls her eyes. "Did you think it'd continue to be like we just started dating?"

I shake my head. "I hoped not. Speaking of which, you should know that I'm looking for something more permanent in Lake Starlight."

I'm still mulling over Kingston's idea to open an indoor youth sports complex in the vacant industrial building just outside of town. I wasn't going to bring up any of my plans to her this morning, but I didn't expect to spend the night having sex with her either.

"I have an appointment to look at a few houses this afternoon. I'd cancel, but this is the only opening the realtor had and Glacier Point is digging into my bank account."

She puts the muffin down on the wrapper in the basket. "We can go. Let me get my dress on so I can do the walk of shame. You can drop me off on your way."

I glance at the clock on the side table. We have two hours before I'm due to meet the realtor. "That's not why I'm telling you."

She turns back to me, holding the blanket to her chest.

"I know this is super early, but I want to know if things between us… is it too early to be looking for a place for all of us?" I ask. Now it's out there. I can't take it back. I just have to wait for her reaction.

She looks into her lap, and her silence kills me. *Way to ruin the morning, Jamison.* I guess we'll be saving that last condom.

"I don't know what to say."

Well, that's not a no. "I shouldn't have asked. I'll just rent a place for now. I don't have to buy right away."

She crawls forward on the bed and sits back on her legs, taking my hand. "It's not that I don't want to share a place with you. But after everything went down with us, I realized how much I relied on you. You were pretty much my sugar daddy."

"Sedona, please never say that again."

She giggles. "I mean you paid for everything for me, and it's not like we were married, or I was a stay-at-home mom. I was young and had a degree. Now I have a travel blog I'm working on. I'm freelancing regularly for magazines. If I were to move in with you, I'd want it to be fifty-fifty."

"Why? We have Palmer now, and you could stay home with her if you want. I'm not sure what I'm going to do, but I have a few things I'm considering." Kingston's offer comes to mind again. Although I have to put up capital for that. But I'm going to sell my condo in New York. That should pay for my house here and then some. I run my hand down the side of her face, tucking a strand of her dark, shiny hair behind her ear. "I like taking care of you."

She nods. "I know you do, but I can't be that girl anymore. The one thing I was sure of before Palmer came into this world was that I wanted to be able to support her on my own. I wanted her to see her mom as a strong, independent woman. I think that's one of the reasons why the postpartum depression made me feel so guilty."

"But—"

She shakes her head. "This isn't up for argument. I'm sure if we never would've broken up, I'd have allowed myself to put my dreams on hold, but I don't want to do that now. I think I'm fortunate to have family to help me. Now I have you, and we can do it together."

"So you want me to rent?"

"I don't want to make that decision for you. If you want to buy, I understand, but for me to move in with you, I want to own half."

I sulk because buying her a house is a dream of mine. I want to get her and Palmer out of that apartment. Give Palmer a huge back yard to run around in, buy her a dog she can play with. The news disappoints me, but at the same time, Sedona's talking about a future between the two of us. That's more than I hoped for and probably more than I deserve. I always thought of Sedona as independent, regardless of whether I was footing the bill for her. None of that ever mattered to me. But I see what it means to her.

"Then I'll rent, and I'll wait for you."

She nods. "I know you're upset, and I'm sorry."

I lean forward and kiss her. "I'm not going to lie, I wish you'd allow me to buy my girls a house, but I understand. We'll work around it."

She locks me to her, holding my cheeks. "Thanks for understanding. I'll still go with you to look at the places though."

I nod. "Want to get Palmer first?"

She smiles. "Definitely. And then we're trading in the man van for an SUV."

"If I can't buy a house, I'm buying a car. We have a big day today."

She laughs and I get her on her back, kissing her.

"I have one more thing we should cross off my list now."

"What's that?" She acts coy.

I hold up the last condom. "We can't leave just one."

"We could save it?"

When I pout, she laughs and snatches it out of my hand, ripping it open with her teeth.

"Damn, I'm hard as a fucking boulder now."

She pushes on my chest and straddles me. Before I know it, my slacks are open and she's rolling a condom down my length and sinking down on me. I rip open her shirt and the buttons fly off, her tits there for me to grab and suckle.

As I watch her chase her pleasure on top of me, I realize that I couldn't love this woman more.

TWENTY-SIX

Sedona

Jamison's realtor is gorgeous. She's got long blonde hair and big blue eyes and a figure I didn't even have before I gave birth. And she thinks it's so adorable how Jamison signs as they converse. Palmer's stuck to him like glue and gives Britani with one T and two I's, all her attention as though she's a Disney princess.

I'm standing nearby in shorts and a T-shirt that says SMILF, courtesy of Phoenix. In the small print, it says Single Mom I'd Like to Fuck, which means it's an open endorsement that we're not married. Maybe Britani thinks Jamison is available.

"You said you used to play soccer, right?" Britani asks Jamison.

"Yeah," he answers and picks up Palmer, following Britani up the walkway.

"That must've been crazy. I can see where things get out of control for sure with that kind of fame. I'll be honest,

I looked you up." She looks at him over her shoulder and flutters her fake eyelashes.

My irritation grows as we approach the house's front door. Her makeup is smeared under her eyes, her hair looks like it hasn't been combed, and her clothes are wrinkled. She's kind of a hot mess. I wasn't going to judge her, especially with what I'm wearing, but now she's openly flirting with my... what is Jamison to me now?

That's a question for a different time.

Regardless, it's clear we share a daughter. That should be enough for her to lay off.

She opens the door—after she puts her ass in Jamison's face by bending over to make sure the key is in the lock properly.

The house is the most modern of the four we've seen so far. It's slightly outside of downtown, closer to where Brooklyn and Wyatt built their home. It's a little too close to Northern Lights Retirement for my liking, but it's not like Grandma Dori rides a bike or anything.

Jamison turns toward me, his face showing his awe, and I look past him and see why. Straight through the house is a wall of windows that overlooks a pond bigger than the one at my parents'... well, Austin and Holly's house. Even from here, I see a dock and a boat.

There's a nice-sized dining room on one side and living room on the other. A staircase that comes from both the foyer and the kitchen connects to the main stairway going upstairs.

Palmer squirms out of Jamison's hold and he lowers her to the floor, where she scurries down the hallway and presses both hands on the glass.

"Just wait until you see what else this house has."

Britani with one T and two I's saunters in front of Jamison, her skirt so tight there's no way in hell she's wearing panties.

Jamison waits for me and puts his hand on the small of my back to go in front of him as we walk down the hallway. Okay, I'm totally jealous for no reason. I've never been one to feel that way with Jamison. I mean, I worried a bit back in the day when he was partying and well known in the soccer circles, but I always looked at it like, I can't stop him, if he wants to screw up what we have, that's his choice. But now after one night together, I want to put a collar around his neck that spells out my name in rhinestones.

Palmer follows Britani to the patio door leading to an in-ground swimming pool and hot tub. I jog ahead and grab Palmer's hand before she can race to the pool's edge and fall into the water.

Britani cringes. "Oh sorry, I'm not used to kids."

No shit.

Jamison picks up Palmer. I can't wait until next week when I'm hoping my heavy lifting restriction is gone. We step outside and I can tell that Jamison is sold on this place. He asks a million questions about having pools in Alaska as though the hot mess express that is Britani is an expert in the field.

I'm salty and irritated, but I need to stop picking on this girl. She hasn't overtly crossed the line. Maybe she's found a little bit of flirting goes a long way with selling houses.

"Palmer, let's go upstairs," I say while signing *upstairs*.

Jamison puts her back down, and the two of us walk through the modern kitchen with quartz countertops and white cabinets to the upstairs master bedroom with the same view as the family room.

It's gorgeous. Damn it. Why can't I already afford half of this place?

Palmer tugs on my arm, pulling me down the hallway. She stops in a room painted pink with a built-in dollhouse in the corner. She sits down and crosses her legs, picking up the small furniture. It seems weird that the dollhouse furniture was left behind since the house is vacant. And I'm pretty sure Jamison will think it's a sign.

"Whoa!" Jamison says. "It's like it was made for her."

"This is such a sweet room. And a dollhouse. Jackpot!" Britani puts her hand in the air for a high five.

I give Jamison a quizzical look and he smirks, walking toward the window. "Another great view. So let me ask you, are they willing to rent?" Jamison turns to face Britani.

And that's my cue to leave. This isn't my business.

I tap Palmer on the shoulder. *Go.*

She shakes her head and picks up the tiny bed, stacking it on another one in the second bedroom of the dollhouse.

I tap her again. *Go now.*

This is the worst. I can't just pick her up and take her out of the room.

Britani says that it's for sale only and she'd have to talk to the listing agent. Jamison says we'd make it worth their while, and I don't even want to know what that means. I want to leave this room, but Palmer is too into the dollhouse to care what I want.

"I'd really prefer a rent-to-buy option," Jamison says.

I tilt my head toward him, and he gives his *yeah, I've got an idea* smile. The same mischievous one that led to us getting caught making out in the janitor's closet in high school, or when he decided he wanted to join me in the changing room when I was trying on swimsuits.

"Britani, can you give me a moment with Sedona, please?"

I want to tell Britani we don't need a moment, that

whatever he's going to try to convince me into isn't happening.

But she starts to leave, then stops at Palmer. "I'll take Palmer."

"No," Jamison and I say in unison.

Whoops.

She startles and looks at us.

"She's good playing with the dollhouse," I say.

Britani walks out the door on her stilettos, but she's doing this weird bounce I think is meant to sway her hips.

After she's gone, I whisper, "Next time, I get to pick out the realtor, okay?"

Jamison disregards my comment. "So I'm thinking we rent this place, you pay me what you pay at your apartment now, and I cover the rest. It'll practically be fifty-fifty, and when we're ready, we buy the owner out."

I cross my arms. "That's not what we discussed."

He shoots me his flirtatious smile. The one that works wonders on almost everyone he encounters.

"Don't," I warn with my finger in his face.

He holds up his hands. "It's just a thought. I'll rent-to-buy it myself, but..." He pulls me into his arms and kisses my neck. "Your rules include sleepovers, right?"

"Sure, Palmer can spend the night." I move to get out of his hold, but his arms tighten.

"I'm not laughing." And he's not.

I know what he wants. He's a "jump in the deep end before you know the temperature of the water" kind of guy. I'm a "put my feet in to test the waters first" kind of girl. Case in point—we're on day one of officially being a couple and we're looking at houses. "Just get it for yourself and we'll talk, okay?"

He presses his lips to mine, and I don't think much of it

until we're being smacked on the legs by two little hands. We look down at Palmer, who is staring at us with furrowed brows. She's never seen us together like this, and she's way too young to understand. She wiggles between us and raises her arms for Jamison to pick her up. Seems someone is jealous. I suppress a grin. Like mother, like daughter.

PALMER LOVES to visit the lake our town is named after. She loves the water and feeding the ducks. Jamison has hung on to this fact to persuade me to move in with him. Somehow Britani sweet-talked the other side into agreeing to a rental that might turn into a buy. In one month, he moves in and he's determined that I move in at the same time.

"Just think, she can feed the ducks every day at the house." He waggles his eyebrows.

Barely an hour goes by without him talking about it.

"Hey, I meant to ask you. Did you ever tell your mom about Palmer?"

His cheery smile disappears, and he picks at the grass. Jamison's parents can be hard on him. His dad used to call him after games and tell him what he needed to improve. When his career ended, I think Jamison's dad wept as much as he did. So I get his reluctance to tell them that there's a child they don't know about. I'm scared that Mum Ferguson will be pissed off at me too.

He picks another blade of grass and wraps it around his finger. "After the car accident, they cut me off for a while."

I don't say anything, keeping my eyes on Palmer.

"They were disappointed that I never came home after my second injury. I'd find my dad in the shed, watching tapes of old games. He couldn't let go of the fact I'd never play professional soccer again. Always bringing up some new treatment that he read about, grasping at anything he thought might hold some promise."

It's weird to hear about what he was doing when we were apart. It's the one section of his life since we met in high school that I don't know about. Except the accident I heard in the press.

"I kept telling him that it was over, but he wouldn't listen. Mum was on me about drinking with my buddies. Dad told her to leave me alone, I was blowing off steam. They'd argue so loud, it'd wake me in the wee hours of the morning with a banging hangover. But I still saw my dad's hope and desperation. If I went into town with him and someone asked about my injury, he'd tell them I'd be good as new, I was just there for a visit while I rehab." Bringing his knees up, he wraps his arms around them. "They want the best for me. I know they do. It's why they had me do the whole foreign exchange student thing." He smiles at me.

I run my hand down his back and slide closer, thankful they did.

"But the pressure from the two of them and my drinking was already so out of control... my dad called this professional in Aberdeen. Some buddy of a buddy. Sent all my scans up there. The day of the accident, the doctor paid us a visit and gave me the news I'd already heard in New York. The chances of me making enough of a recovery to play again were slim. I wouldn't be able to keep up with the athleticism, and if I did, it would only be a short time before I injured myself again. The look on my dad's face was tragic. It was like watching myself get the news the first time all over again. After the doctor left, my dad retreated to the shed, and I went to the pub. Got smashed and well..." He glances at me. "You know the rest."

I nod and lay my head on his shoulder.

"They kicked me out of the house. That was rock bottom for me. I'd already lost you and our daughter, my career, my parents, and the press had a hold of the story. I returned to the U.S. and got clean. Part of my rehab was to make amends. After some hard conversations, my mum was happy, but my dad still mourns my career. We're civil, but nothing more. To tell them that I hid their first grandchild from them... I feel like a disappointment all over again."

When a duck gets too close, Palmer runs to us. Jamison opens his arms, and she falls into them. He lies on his back and has her fly up above him. I lie down too, looking at her, and Jamison lowers her so she's half on me and half on him. We put our arms around our daughter and both kiss one of her cheeks.

After we pack up and we're folding the blanket, I know I have to say something to try to fix this situation. "I'll gladly tell them you didn't know about her."

His eyes widen, but he shakes his head. "I can't have others fixing problems for me, but I love you for offering." He presses his lips to mine. I'd love for the kiss to be longer, but our daughter slides between us again. "This is something I have to handle on my own."

I nod and hope this isn't the catalyst that could drive him to drink again.

TWENTY-SEVEN

Jamison

I leave the AA meeting in Sunrise Bay and dial-up Merrick on my way to my minivan. After I pick up Sedona, we're turning in the rental and I'm going to buy my own SUV.

"Hey, man," he says. "How are things?"

"They're good. I'm renting a house I hope to buy down the road, and I'm on my way to pick up Sedona to buy myself a car."

He's silent for a second. "That's a lot of change. You ready for all this? You do know that just because you missed part of their lives, you don't have to make it all up at once."

Merrick probably assumes the spontaneous side of me, the one that thinks of consequences after the fact, is ruling me right now, but this is something I always wanted. Ever since I left Sedona to play in the Scottish Premier League, I've dreamed of having a family with her.

"I know. But I want this. This is where I belong." I decide

not to tell him that I've agreed to Kingston's idea about starting a youth sports complex where we combine our talents and I teach soccer and he teaches baseball. That might take Merrick right over the edge and he'll fly out to Alaska. "There's actually something I've wanted to talk to you about."

"What's that?"

"Do you think I'm good enough to be a sponsor?"

Another beat of silence. Merrick is a "think about his words before he uses them" kind of guy. "You've been sober for over a year, and yes, I think you could help someone work through their steps."

I want to help someone the way Merrick helped me, and it's not like I'm crazy busy at the moment. Plus, the leader of my usual AA group asked today, and I know some of our members are struggling.

"So you think I should do it? There's a need for one where I've been going to meetings."

"Yeah, give it a try, but you have to be ready to say it's not a good fit. Sometimes a pair doesn't jive for no reason other than they don't. So keep that in mind. You have a good heart, Jamie, and I don't want you to suffer a downward spiral and go down a bad road because you couldn't help someone the way you wanted to. Remember this disease affects people differently."

I was damn lucky to get Merrick as my sponsor. The guy's been sober for almost seven years, and he had a slip up right before that when he'd been sober for five. You just never know. But he's a success, in my opinion.

"Okay. I'm going to say yes."

"And you have to be able to drop things for them if they call. Will Sedona understand?" I hadn't thought about that, but... Merrick interrupts my thoughts. "You can't tell her who you're sponsoring either. They have to remain anonymous as well. Just things to consider."

I've already kept to myself the fact that we both know one person who attends the meetings with me.

I nod, although he can't see me. "Got it. Thanks, Merrick."

"Call me whenever. And slow down a little. Enjoy this time with you and your family together again."

I laugh. "Okay."

"Yeah, whatever, Andretti."

I laugh and say my goodbye.

Driving over to Sedona's, my stomach flutters with excitement. I think I'm finally back on the right path in my life.

PALMER'S NAPPING when I arrive, but Sedona's wearing a tight tank top and a pair of shorts that immediately make my pants feel tight.

"You mind listening for her while I shower?" She walks into the bedroom and I follow.

"That means I can't join you." I wrap my arms around her stomach, behind her at the bed's edge.

"Sorry."

I fiddle with the hem of her shirt and inch it up, exposing her stomach. She still flinches when I touch her stomach, and it's not because she's in pain. It's because she's self-conscious. I hate that.

"I can at least undress you." I inch it up some more and she raises her hands, allowing me to pull off the shirt and toss it onto the floor. I groan at the sports bra underneath. "I hate these things."

She laughs, and I'm fairly sure we're remembering when I showed up in New York all those years ago. "Practice makes perfect. You had this down a few years ago."

She's right. When we started working out together, I did become a master at the sports bra removal, but I'm rusty now. She keeps her arms in the air and she leans back into me. I pull the fabric up over her head, and my reward is her bare tits begging for my hands.

Dropping her arms, she places her hands over mine, which are molded to her tits. "Way to go, Ferguson."

"I guess it's like riding a bike," I mumble and kiss the shell of her ear. "Now for the shorts." My tongue glides down her spine as I hunch to push her shorts down to her ankles. She steps out of them, and my hands slide up her torso as I make my way back up her body. "I need to be inside you."

She moans and turns around. "I'm a sweaty mess. I have a better idea."

She falls to her knees in front of me, unbuttoning my jeans and sliding the zipper down while her gaze meets mine. There's no better sight than this one.

She frees my cock, pushing my jeans and boxers down my legs to pool at my ankles. When she urges me back to spin around, I fall onto the bed and she situates herself between my thighs. We explored together enough as teenagers that Sedona knows what makes me tick. She learned what I enjoy when she's blowing me until she got it down to a damn art. I can come in two minutes when her mouth is on me. But it's been so long, I fear I'll come the minute she runs her tongue up my length.

My hips jut out and I rise off the bed from the sensation of her warm, inviting mouth. My breathing labors the farther she sucks me down, and I watch her take half my dick into her mouth. My fists clench the comforter and I groan, closing my eyes.

"Damn it, lass," I say, mentally reminding myself she's always been this good. Some new guy didn't teach her anything. I was just more used to it back then.

I hang on by a thread until her free hand dips down and plays with my balls. Just like that, it's game over. My hand threads through her hair and I hold her to me as I pump into her mouth. I'd hoped to last longer because it feels fucking fantastic and I don't want it to end, but I can't hold off any longer. It's been so long since she's worked her magic on me. I pour into her with a groan.

She rises to her feet and I kiss her hard. Tasting myself on her lips makes me hard all over again.

"I better shower," she mumbles against my lips.

"Please let me join you," I whine like a child.

"Sorry, you're on daddy duty. But maybe tonight after she goes to bed…"

I pull her to me again, my tongue diving into her mouth, never satisfied. "You better believe it. So can I spend the night?"

She hesitates. Since the SunBay Inn, we haven't spent the night together because we're not sure how to navigate it with Palmer. I'm not even sure Palmer will notice. I'm here every night when she goes to bed and usually shortly after she wakes up.

"I suppose we could bend the rules."

My hands mold to her ass. "I promise you won't regret that decision."

She laughs, wiggling out of my hold. "Time for me to shower."

For the first time, she struts naked in front of me, and she coyly glances at me over her shoulder before disappearing into the bathroom. It takes all my restraint not to follow her.

"THAT'S HER," I say to Sedona as we park outside the car rental place. I've delayed returning the van because I feel like an ass.

"Are you actually scared?" she asks, her eyebrows high on her head.

"You should've heard her. She was so mad and disappointed."

I retold Sedona the story on the way over here, fully aware I sounded like a scorned child. What do I care what this woman thinks of me? I shouldn't. Only two women are important to me, and they're in this minivan with me. Well, and my mum.

"Oh please." Sedona takes the keys out of the ignition. "Get Palmer."

She opens her door, feet landing on the pavement. I get out, unstrap Palmer, and take the car seat out of the minivan, fully aware something is going down. When I set the car seat to the side of the minivan, Kingston pulls into the parking lot to pick us up.

Sedona opens the door of the rental place, and Gina looks up at her from behind the counter.

"What's the hold-up?" he asks, climbing out of his truck.

"Grab some popcorn. There's gonna be a show."

I rush Palmer to go inside because I haven't seen Sedona look this determined to put someone in their place since the time I had a crazy fan who didn't know the meaning of personal space. Kingston comes in alongside us.

Sedona slams the keys on the counter. "He's returning this."

Gina looks past Sedona at me. "Okay. Well, he needs to sign the paperwork."

Sedona turns to me, and Kingston takes Palmer's hand so I can join them. Gina quietly gets the paperwork together and I sign all the documents.

"I have to inspect the outside of it. Just in case you were in an accident." Gina's sneer is deliberate, and Sedona sighs, following her out. "Sometimes people don't realize they bump into thinks like light poles and signs."

Now we're all outside, Kingston and Palmer included. Kingston is doing his best to sign what's being said to Palmer though he misses a lot of it. I smile because it will only help her even if she doesn't understand all the signs yet.

"Does that happen a lot?" Sedona asks.

Gina looks up from her iPad and back at me. "Some people think they're special."

I cannot believe this woman is still acting like this. So I step forward, ready to lower my voice. I should have never let her intimidate me to the point that I wouldn't return the minivan until now.

But Sedona's hand lands on my chest and she steps up in front of me. "I'm not sure who you think you are, but this man right here is amazing."

Gina huffs and rolls her eyes. She goes inside to the office and we all follow.

Sedona looks Gina up and down, saying in a judgmental tone, "He made a mistake. Lots of people do. Maybe you're familiar with the concept."

"Let's just go. King, stop signing," I say.

"Why? We're helping Palmer," he says, his fingers not stopping.

Sedona shrugs out of my hold on her upper arm. "I'm not going anywhere. You can't talk to people like that. He's a human being. I know he's some huge celebrity in your eyes and I'm sorry that what he did disappointed your son, but believe me, he carries the burden of that every day. But he's human—he fucked up, and he's worked hard to get back to a good place in his life."

"Well, I don't know how to sign that word," Kingston says from behind us. "Probably for the best. I'll just say you made a mistake."

I shake my head. I should've done this myself—not that it doesn't feel good to watch Sedona defend me.

"When he's getting paid all that money, he has a responsibility to his fans," Gina says.

Sedona throws her hands in the air. "Are you kidding me? He's fucking human."

"You're making this hard, Sedona," Kingston says.

"Just because he's so talented in soccer doesn't mean he lives his life for you. All you know about him is what you read in gossip magazines." Sedona looks behind us, where Kingston bites his lip while Palmer waits intently for him to sign. But Sedona picks up Palmer and turns her toward the woman. "This girl is the luckiest girl in this world to call this man daddy. He's gentle and kind and loves her with his whole heart. So from now on, why don't you keep your judgments to yourself? You don't know him, and you don't know our family."

Palmer squirms to get free, and Sedona sets her down. I move to get her, but Palmer goes to a desk on the side of the counter, picks up a coffee mug, and chucks it at the lady.

Gina darts to the side to prevent her leg from being hit. "Great work on your kid. I see the apple didn't fall far."

Sedona rushes the desk, but I hold her back, bringing her into my arms.

Kingston grabs Palmer, picking her up, and chuckles. "Oh shit. I told you she's been hanging around Savannah and Brinley too much."

"Let's just go before we're in Buzz Wheel for a fight in the rental car shop," I whisper. "She's not worth it."

Sedona calms but turns around once more. "You're right, King. I guess you need to work with her on her aim."

Kingston belts out a huge laugh and I chuckle. Sedona snatches Palmer out of Kingston's arms and bolts from the place.

"Shit, man, if that's not a declaration of love, I don't know what is." Kingston pats me on the back as we walk out of the rental place.

Damn, my heart was already floating out of my chest from being with her, but now I'm riding sky-high.

TWENTY-EIGHT

Sedona

"So he's renting a house but really he wants to buy it?" Phoenix rolls her eyes and walks a beat faster.

I put my hand on her arm. "Can we please slow down? I just got my okay to exercise last week."

We're walking on the path along the water in Sunrise Bay for a change of scenery, me pushing Palmer in a stroller while she naps. My sister has been in LA, and this is my first time seeing her since Jamison and I got back together. As expected, she's not thrilled about the news.

"Explain it to me again. Ethel and Grandma fixed you up, and so you just slept with him." She raises her hand before I can answer. "Please, for the love of God, tell me you used protection."

"Yeah, there was a box of condoms in the welcome basket."

She stops cold and I take the opportunity to catch my breath. "You didn't?"

"I told you I slept with him. I told you we're a couple now."

"No, I mean you didn't use the condoms they supplied, did you?" Her face indicates she's thinking *you cannot be this stupid, Sedona*.

"What were we going to do?"

"They probably put a pinprick in them." She stares at my stomach as if I'm already growing a baby inside.

I cover my stomach with my hand. "I doubt it."

She widens her eyes and walks again. "You know how much she loves to brag about how many great-grandchildren she has. Just sayin'."

I look down at my belly for a second. No. Definitely not.

"Where is Mr. Wonderful anyway?" She looks like those mall walkers, hips swaying, arms that could injure a passerby.

"Not sure. He just said he'd be by for dinner. Did you know he's coaching Calista's soccer team now?"

I'm not going to say anything—because I'm on Operation Get Phoenix to Like Jamison—but the last few days have been odd. He's not hanging out at my apartment as much as usual and he canceled on me last night, saying he was tired. A pit in my stomach says something isn't right. Maybe he's mad that I won't move in with him? Feels like I'm giving him the cold shoulder?

I've never ignored my gut, and I'm not going to now. Jamison has never given me a reason to be jealous. Ever. Even when I was anyway. So I'm trying to give him space, but I think I'm going to ask him about it at dinner tonight. We have to live our lives like an open book, and if something is going on with him, we need to discuss it whether it's difficult or not.

"Hmm," she murmurs.

"Will you please stop it? We're giving it an honest shot, and you, as my sister, need to be on my side."

"I'm on your side, just not his."

I struggle to keep up with her. "That's it, you're taking the stroller."

She stops ten paces in front of me and waits for me to catch up with Palmer. I hand it off to her and keep going.

"Oh, this is good. More of a challenge than just walking," she says.

"Thanks for making me feel like a complete loser."

She pats my back. "You just had a baby. I have no idea what that's like. I might soon though."

I stumble a step. "Is there something you have to tell me?"

She gets that look in her eye. The devilish one after she's done something bad.

"I'm pregnant," she whispers loud enough for me to hear.

"What?" I screech and stop on the trail.

People behind us mumble and go around me.

"Shh!" She walks again and I have to try to pry my jaw up from dragging along the asphalt. "The worst part is that now Griffin wants to marry me."

"That's a bad thing?"

Phoenix shrugs. "I don't want him to marry me just because he knocked me up. What if Mr. Wonderful had proposed to you when you were preggo with Palmer?"

Truthfully, I thought he would. I wouldn't have thought twice about it. But he didn't. "I don't know."

"What if he proposed to you now?"

"He asked me to move into the house with him."

Now she stops, and I welcome the break to inhale a full breath. "And you said no?"

"Yeah." I take another labored breath. "I don't want to rely on him anymore. I want my own money and independence, which means, to me, living in a place I pay for. At least for a while."

She punches my shoulder. "Way to go. Stick it to him."

"I'm not sticking it to him."

"You kind of are. I'm sure he wants to just pick up where you two left off and forget how much he fucked up."

Spotting a bench, I take the stroller from her and detour to it.

She follows me. "What's the deal? I cannot let this baby ruin my figure. I gotta workout during the pregnancy and right after."

I roll my eyes. The joys of being a pop star. "I'm not walking with you. In fact, I'm not going to talk to you anymore."

"What are we, six again and I cut your Barbie's hair?" She does lunges in front of the bench.

She's so annoyingly in shape. Talk about feeling bad about where your body is at. Try having a twin who's like staring at a picture of your old self live and in person.

"I love him, Phoenix. I always have. My reasons for not moving in with him have nothing to do with any doubts. I'm the one he scorned, and if I can forgive him, you need to as well." I cross my legs and my arms.

Her eyes roll so hard, I'm surprised they come back around to stare at me. "Ugh. Fine. It's just he hurt you so much."

"I know, but life is too short, and he's Palmer's father. I need to forgive and forget for myself and my daughter. You need to as well." She jogs in place and I watch with annoyance. "Can we talk about you and Griffin now?"

"There's nothing to say. He wants to get married and I said no."

"Phoenix," I sigh. "Why?"

She gives me an expression that says I should already know this. "Because he feels obligated. I'm not getting married just because we got drunk one night and had sex without protection." She does lunges again.

"The man loves you. Have you told Maverick you're pregnant yet?"

"No. We're waiting the full three months before we tell anyone." She points at me. "So mum is the word, blabbermouth."

"Blabbermouth? I keep all your damn secrets."

She blows out a breath and shakes her head. "Everyone knows it's only Rome who keeps secrets in this family. So if word gets out, I'm coming after you."

"Are you excited about the pregnancy though?"

A large smile transforms her face. "Excited and nervous."

"You'll be a great mom." Unable to see her working out anymore, I stand. "Let's get this over with. I'm tired."

"Tired from too much sex?" Phoenix elbows me.

We get back on the path and I peek in the stroller to see Palmer is still out. "It is nice to get it on the regular." I fight the smile that wants to come out.

"There's something to be said for when you know each other so well. Nothing like wasting time with a guy who can't use his tongue properly or someone who's crazy attractive but just cannot give you what you need."

I keep to myself the fact that I wouldn't know. Jamison

has been my only partner. But I love having sex with him, and I don't feel as if I'm missing anything.

Phoenix nods at the stroller. "And how is Palmer handling him being around so much?"

"She loves it. She loves him. You should see how she looks at him."

She nods. "Sucker."

"Phoenix, I'm serious. This has to stop. You have to stop saying things like that. I'm with him, and you need to push your negativity away. It's my life and my decision. I don't agree with you saying no to Griffin's proposal, but you won't see me making comment after comment about it."

Her face softens and her pace slows. "Well then, explain that to me?" Phoenix nods to the right.

I turn to see Britani with one T and two I's crying in my boyfriend's arms.

TWENTY-NINE

Jamison

I've been keeping a secret from Sedona and it sucks. I never intended to. Everything just snowballed and now I have to figure out how to get out of this.

"Everything crumbled around me. How can they just act like I'm not their daughter?" Britani's hand lands on my thigh.

I glance around. We might be in Sunrise Bay, but I've seen things that happened in other cities show up in Buzz Wheel.

"It's hard to accept, but you have no control over their reaction. You can only control your own," I say, but my thoughts aren't on her. They're on Sedona. If she saw this scene, she wouldn't understand.

"I'm their daughter. Can they honestly just not forgive me?" she cries.

My heart squeezes because I can empathize with how she feels, but I'm not comfortable having her draped all over me.

An elderly couple walking down the path side-eyes us. The walking and biking path is booming today. After my AA meeting, Britani and I came down here because I've decided to offer to be her sponsor. But she won't stop touching or hugging me, and I don't feel comfortable with it.

"Most times, once the addiction hits rock bottom, the family is done. It's not to say they don't love you. But you'll get through this. In time, when they see that you've taken control of your life, perhaps they'll change their minds."

She looks at me as if I hung the moon. Fuck me. Then she's in my arms and crying some more. She's clinging to me like a damn koala bear and I pat her back awkwardly.

"*Phoenix!*"

I turn. As I feared, there isn't a different Phoenix in Sunrise Bay—it's my girl's devil twin sister, sprinting toward me with a murderous look in her eye.

Britani has no idea what's happening and no way of preparing herself before Phoenix stands in front of us with her hands on her hips. Sedona joins us, Palmer asleep in the stroller. But then Sedona hits a bump and Palmer's head jostles, waking her.

Phoenix kicks me in the shin. "You son of a bitch!"

"Phoenix, stop it," Sedona says, but I don't miss the hurt in her eyes.

"I will not. For the past hour, you've been working me to forgive him and look at him now. With some chick on a park bench in a neighboring community. How convenient. At least you were smart enough not to put your full level of douchebag on display in Lake Starlight."

I dislodge myself from Britani.

"This isn't what it looks like." I speak only to Sedona.

Palmer whines in her seat, and when she sees me, she flails her arms to get out.

"You can't even come up with an original line?" Phoenix steps between Sedona and me, blocking Palmer from seeing me.

It's going to get ugly if Phoenix thinks she'll keep me from my daughter.

"What is going on?" Sedona asks.

Thank God I'm with the rational twin who will hear me out.

I look at Britani and back at Sedona. I can't tell Sedona everything because of the anonymity guidelines of Alcoholics Anonymous. "I'm just helping her with something. She's going through a hard time."

"And she doesn't have anyone else to hold her and wipe her tears?" Phoenix puts her hands on her hips.

"I wasn't wiping her tears." I turn to Britani. "Give me a moment with Sedona, okay?"

Britani stands and grabs her purse. "I have a meeting to show the new condos that went up along the bay anyway." She acts as though she's got her life figured out and waves to Palmer as she leaves.

"Don't wave to her," Phoenix says.

Britani laughs.

Phoenix moves to follow her, but Sedona stops her. "Give us a minute."

Phoenix points at me. "You're scum."

"You have no idea what yer talking about," I say.

"Just go for a walk," Sedona tells Phoenix, pushing the stroller over to her.

Phoenix takes the stroller and heads to the path where she walks away with Palmer in the opposite direction Britani took. That's a small relief.

Sedona stands there, not kissing or hugging me hello. The wedge between us has returned.

"Will you sit?" I ask.

She sits, but on the opposite side of the bench. I blow out a breath.

"Is she just your realtor?" she asks, picking at her nails.

I slide closer to her, laying my arm along the back of the bench. "No. I met her somewhere. Somewhere where people stay anonymous."

She looks at me, and instead of understanding, there's sorrow. I don't share much about my recovery with Sedona because after our dinner date, I realized she felt that I chose my disease over her. It couldn't be further from the truth, but I respect the way she feels.

She looks at the ground. "Oh. You probably have a lot in common."

"We do. Most of us do. We tend to fuck up our lives. She's new to the program and I thought I'd support her like my sponsor did me so that her chances of success would be better. I used her as a realtor to help her too. I couldn't and shouldn't tell you, because she should remain anonymous, but I can't allow you to think this was anything but me helping someone who's going through something I'm keenly familiar with."

She turns her head and looks at me. "It's funny. I was never that jealous when you were a big deal in the soccer world. You'd travel, and sure, there would be rumors, especially with Johnny around."

Johnny was a teammate and a cheater. Never faithful, but he was always a lot of fun to be around.

"But those last months when you didn't come home at night and you'd show up so drunk in the morning... I wondered if there were other women. That maybe you were so out of it, you did cheat."

"I never—"

She holds up her hand. "You don't have to sell me on it. It's in the past and I believe you. It wasn't you then, it was your disease, and I've made peace with that. But right now when Phoenix saw you... at first, my heart lurched. Mostly because when we went to look for houses with Britani, the whole time, all I could do was compare myself to her. The fact she didn't just give birth. As bad as she was with Palmer, I assume she hasn't lived through two pregnancies. Her body is toned and fit, and here I am, barely able to keep up with my twin on a walk around the bay."

My heart squeezes when I hear her compare herself to Britani. Why can't she see what I see? My fingers run along her shoulder and upper arm. "Yer so beautiful. Never think yer not the hottest woman in the room."

She grins and points at me. "See, that's why the minute you pushed her away and stood, I knew you wouldn't do that to Palmer and me. I mean, you've come this far. You wouldn't just cheat on me. Something inside told me whatever was happening with Britani was innocent. That my insecurities around her are my problem, not yours."

"Really?" I hate the surprise in my tone over the fact that she believes me.

"Don't get me wrong, for a quick second, I did want to take her by her bleach-blonde hair and throw her in the bay, but I saw it in your eyes. The fear that you'd lose Palmer and me."

"I really want to kiss you," I say, bending forward and putting my hand on her cheek to pull her toward me.

"Okay."

I press my lips to hers, my pulse igniting when our tongues touch. Our kiss grows a little too sexual for daytime at a park.

"Here's your daughter. Get a room. And my sister might believe you, but I do not," Phoenix says and walks away.

I close the kiss and my forehead falls to hers. "How on Earth did I get so lucky to get you?"

"Twice, at that," she says.

"I'm the luckiest man in the world."

"And never forget it."

The next day, I tell Britani I can't be her sponsor. Although I want to help people, I can't risk my own life and sobriety when I just got them back.

"HERE THEY ARE," Kingston says. "Our first team. I hate to sound like the proud uncle, but Calista's the best we got."

"Let's teach them how to kick a ball first, I suppose."

We watch the ten girls try to kick a soccer ball around the pitch. We're outside right now, but once the building is ready, we'll move indoors when the colder weather hits. Although Kingston's specialty will be baseball, we're mid-season and he'll never get enough people until the fall at the earliest. Since Calista said she wanted to learn soccer and had some friends that did too, we're going to start a camp that might play a few local teams.

We spend the next half hour trying to show the girls the right way to kick a ball.

Midway through practice, I spot Calista signing to a girl in Kingston's group. I saw her hearing aids when she arrived but figured she could hear well enough since her parents didn't mention anything to us.

I pull Calista to the side. "Nicole's deaf?"

"She can read lips pretty well, but she's hard of hearing. She sometimes has an interpreter with her in class."

Calista's feet keep moving on the ball and I wonder what Rome will think about his daughter being a soccer player instead of a softball one.

"That's why you've been so interested in signing?"

She laughs. "Yeah, but also for Palmer. I can't imagine what it's like to not know what people are talking about."

I wrap my arm around her shoulders and kiss her temple. "Yer a good person, you know that?"

"Tell my mom and dad that, will you?" She smiles and runs off to join the group of girls.

After practice, I sit down in the middle of the pitch.

Kingston falls to his back beside me. "I think I saw some improvement today."

"Yeah." A part of me wonders what it would be like to coach professionals. To be teaching strategy instead of showing kids how to kick a ball between passes and how to score a goal.

"You miss it?" he asks.

"Why do you ask?"

He points at my face. "It's all over your face. Maybe you need to stay away from the sport totally. What if it sends you spiraling?"

"I wouldn't let it come to that." I shrug. "Don't you miss baseball?"

"No. That was never my calling. I love teaching the kids though. Last year, Rome put Dion in tee-ball, and it was a thrill to see those little guys find the love of the game. The joy in their eyes when they hit the ball."

Sadly, I don't relate. I didn't feel that today, but maybe I'm just feeling sorry for myself. Professional coaching announcements are due in a few weeks, and before I knew settling here with Sedona and Palmer was an option, I'd hoped my name would be on the list.

"Here comes trouble." Kingston points at Sedona and Palmer walking with Stella.

Palmer runs into me, knocking me back to the ground. Yeah, I wouldn't change a damn thing.

"How about some pizza?" Stella suggests, cozying up with Kingston on the grass.

He rolls them over so he's on top of her, and I cover Palmer's eyes.

"Get a room," I say.

"You're just jealous because you have little eyes on you all the time," Kingston says with a grin.

I lean forward and kiss Sedona. Palmer places one hand on the backs of our heads to keep us kissing.

"He's right," I mumble against her lips.

"Yeah, I'm slightly jealous, but I still wouldn't be humping on the soccer field," Sedona says.

"I can't help it. She's just so damn edible." Kingston pretends to attack Stella's neck like a vampire.

I sign to Palmer. *Climb Uncle. On his back.*

She smiles and takes my advice, catapulting herself on top of him. He easily climbs off of Stella and swings Palmer around, throwing her up in the air. Sedona cuddles up next to me as Stella laughs.

Who would've thought we'd all end up here? Although there's one Bailey I haven't won over yet, I couldn't be happier. That is, until Sedona leans closer and puts her hand on my stomach.

"It's time to call your mom," she whispers.

Yeah, there's still that boulder to roll over.

THIRTY

Sedona

I sit next to Jamison as his shaking hands dial his mom's number. He puts it on speaker. Palmer is sleeping, so we have plenty of time.

She answers on the first ring. "Jamie?"

"Hey, Mum," he says.

"Where're you at, lad? New York?"

This shows how much they haven't stayed in contact. There was a time he called home every Sunday.

"I'm actually in Lake Starlight." He looks at me, and I grab his hand.

"Oh, okay. And Sedona?"

"She's here too. I actually have you on speaker with her."

"Nice." I hear her sewing machine in the background. She's always busy doing something. "Ye two together?"

Again he looks at me. "Yeah, we are. But there's something I need to tell you."

"What is it?" Her voice becomes alarmed. "Trouble again?"

"No. Not that."

"Oh good. Your father would not be happy."

"I know. It's something else. Something I didn't tell you but should have."

"What's this?" Her voice comes across gruff. It even scares me a little.

"Um."

"Oh, for goodness' sake, spit it out, Jamie. Nothing good comes from secrets. I've told ye that since ye were a little one, but you were always keeping secrets."

Jamison blows out a breath and I squeeze his hand harder. "I have a daughter."

"What?" His mom's voice lowers, and it's laced with weariness.

"Sedona was pregnant when I got injured. You have a granddaughter. Her name is—"

Click. The line goes dead.

Jamison drops the phone. "See. I told you. Why did I even try?"

My phone rings from across the room on the charger. I leave Jamison and grab it, seeing his mom's name. I hold it up to him.

"She must be really pissed with me if she's calling you for details," he says.

I shrug but slide over the screen with my thumb. "Hello?" I answer with as much calm as I can.

I haven't ever called his mom. She's definitely a blood-is-thicker type of woman, so when I left Jamison, I was dead to her.

"Sedona?"

"Yes?"

"Is it true?"

I put the phone on speaker so Jamison can hear her. "It is."

"How old is the lass?"

"She's twenty months."

"Oh God. And she doesn't even know her grannie or granda."

Jamison puts his head in his hands as I sit next to him. "She'd love to get to know you. She's very sweet and loving. Her name is Palmer."

"Palmer Ferguson. A good solid name."

Then it dawns on me—I didn't give her Jamison's last name. All this time he's been back in our lives and I didn't even think about it. As though it had never occurred to Jamison either, he looks at me, clearly questioning if his mom is correct.

"Um... technically she's Palmer Bailey, but..."

Jamison stands, hurt in his eyes, and goes into my bedroom, quietly shutting the door.

"Oh, so you and Jamie weren't together?"

"No, not at the time, but we are now. We're happy. Very happy."

"That's good. Will you send me pictures?"

"Of course. Give me a moment." I go to my photos and open up a text exchange. I send her a few of Palmer alone by the ducks and one of Palmer and Jamison together.

"Hold on. I'm getting yer message." There's nothing for a moment until I hear sniffles. "She's beautiful."

My heart aches to be with Jamison right now. To fix Palmer's legal name now that he's a part of her life. "There's something else you need to know as well."

"Oh Lord, I'm bracing myself."

"She's deaf."

"Oh, I can sign," she says with more excitement in her tone. "My brother was deaf. He's passed now, but I'm sure I still know my signs. I'll practice."

I chuckle, then silence falls over the phone. "That's great. Jamison is much more fluent in signing than me. He's done amazing things for her. You'd be really proud."

More silence. The strain between them is deeper than I thought.

"He's good. Healthy? Staying away from the drink?"

"Yep. He's really good. Doing all the work he needs to in order to stay sober."

"Ye know, I blame meself. My family likes the drink. I shoulda watched him better."

Oh, how familiar I am with the mom guilt. "He's good. I promise."

"He looks good in the picture you sent me. Strong again. He was so frail and thin."

Jamison comes out of the bedroom and sits beside me, having gathered himself.

"Would you like to talk to him?"

"Only if he wants to talk to me."

I hand Jamison the phone.

"Hey, Mum," he says.

I pat his leg and grab my laptop before going into the bedroom to give him the privacy he needs. Opening my computer, I search for how to get Palmer's last name changed to Ferguson. After printing the forms I need, I return to my bedroom and fill them out.

Jamison comes in twenty minutes later. "She's going to come for a visit now, you know."

"I know, or maybe we go there."

He sits down on the bed. "She sounds happy. I thought maybe we'd FaceTime her with Palmer after she wakes up."

I push away the papers. "Definitely. Palmer will love her. Other than Dori, she doesn't have a grandma or a grandpa in her life."

He nods. "Give me time on the grandpa thing."

"Okay."

I move to straddle him and wrap my legs around his waist. He sits quietly. "I'm really proud of you."

"Thanks. When she hung up on me..." He shakes his head.

I laugh then say with my best Scottish accent—which is pretty lame—"I love your mum."

He flips me over on my back. "Are you mocking me?"

"No way. But how about you grab your kilt?"

I remember how much Phoenix once annoyed him with that stereotype. He tickles me but I squirm, and his lips end up on mine, his knee nudging apart my thighs. As he devours my neck and I grab the hem of his T-shirt, he picks up one of the papers crinkling under my back.

"What's this?"

I sit up and stack them in a pile before putting them on my nightstand. "It's a petition to change Palmer's last name to Ferguson."

His shoulders sink and he glances at me through his long dark eyelashes. "You don't have to."

I crawl up his lap and put my finger to his lips. "At the time, I just couldn't imagine always explaining to everyone why we had different last names. I didn't want to remember you every time I told someone her name or filled out a form. It was too painful. But you are her father and if I wasn't in so much pain, I would've put your last name down regardless of whether we were together or not."

His arms wind around my back. "I'm never leaving you."

"I know, and that's why I want to do this for you."

"Thank you." He kisses me. "Now I just need to get you to be a Ferguson too." He lays me down on the bed.

"Slow down there." I laugh, allowing him to slide my shirt up my stomach.

"Want to work on baby number two?"

I clear my throat. "You really don't know the meaning of slow, do you?"

He pulls my shirt off me. "When it comes to you? No. Well, other than trying to savor you until I combust."

The weight of his body falls over me and he situates himself between my legs, grinding his long length into my core. "I love you, Sedona Bailey Ferguson."

I slap his shoulder.

"One day. One day we'll be the Fergusons and I'll be talking to your swollen belly because we're going to be a family."

I shake my head, but he's right. One day. I just don't know how he's so sure he wants us to jump in so deep so fast. Then again, it's one of the reasons I love him. He left soccer in Scotland to come to the MLS just to be with me. The first thing he did after getting sober was seek me out.

Finally, it dawns on me that he's been preparing for this moment for months. While I was waiting for him to desert me again, he was planning our resurrection. He always had faith. I could learn a little something from him.

THIRTY-ONE

Jamison

Three weeks pass, and we're seeing progress in our young soccer team.

Calista runs down the field and passes to Kaylee, who passes to Ava up by the net. She kicks the ball and it goes right in past Kingston. A legit goal. Calista and the girls all run and hug one another, jumping up and down.

I smile and Kingston looks over them at me, his expression showing he's impressed.

It *is* impressive that after only three weeks, we've seen this much progress.

"Great job, girls." I clap. "We've got five minutes left but you worked hard so why don't you hang out until yer parents get here."

Calista weaves to look around me, then signs *hello, I'm happy you're here.*

I turn, expecting to find Nicole, but it's Palmer. She's kicking her own ball toward me. Yep, she'll be a soccer star. I'll make sure of it.

Nicole runs down the field toward my daughter. I think she feels a bond with Palmer—probably because they're different in similar ways.

All of the girls sit down with Palmer, fawning over her. They all sign *a little bit* to her because Calista and Nicole have been teaching them some basics.

Palmer signs back. *Play.*

I glance behind me, and I'm disappointed not to find Sedona, but Harley. Dion runs from her and takes the ball we were using down the field and scores on Kingston—although in King's defense, he was on his phone.

"You're a natural," Kingston says.

Harley comes over with Linus in her arms and a pouting Phoebe by her side.

Kingston walks past the girls huddled together over to us. "What's up with her?"

"She wanted Stella to be here," Harley says.

She lets down Linus and he joins Palmer. The two of them have something like a sibling bond, because they were born so close to each other.

"What's up, LJ?" Kingston puts his hand up for a high five.

"Will you please stop calling him that?" Harley says.

"Believe me, you want this nickname to stick. You're just asking for his ass to end up in a locker with the name Linus."

"It's a great name," Harley says.

Kingston sighs and his gaze zeroes in on her belly. My attention fell there too, but I didn't want to say anything. The worst thing you can do is ask a woman whether she's pregnant or not.

But Kingston points. "What's going on there?"

Harley looks down to where her shirt has ridden up a little since it's stretched out. "Don't worry about it."

"You cannot be pregnant again," King says. "Seriously, I'm going to pick up Rome and drive him to get fixed myself."

She shoots him a glare. "This is none of your business. And you shouldn't be making me feel ashamed that I'm pregnant, okay? You came from a family of nine." Harley yanks her shirt down.

I step forward and kiss her cheek. "Congratulations."

"See." She points at Kingston. "That's how you should be. Not so judgy."

Kingston wraps his arms around her and exaggerates a kiss on her cheek. "Congrats, sis, another baby. Do you think the spark will ever die?"

"Is your spark dead? Stella isn't pregnant yet?" Harley raises an eyebrow.

"No, because we use protection."

She throws her hands in the air, obviously exasperated.

Kingston laughs since we all know Harley and Rome use protection too. It just never works. "Were you hoping to keep this one quiet?"

Her jaw shifts and I'd bet money she's going to hit him. "Every pregnancy, my baby bulge shows sooner. I'm only nine weeks along."

"Twins!" Kingston punches me in the arm. "I'm calling it right now. You're my witness. You've got twins coming."

She looks at her stomach with wide eyes for a moment, then cringes.

"One of us has to get them. It makes more sense for one of the actual twins to have them." He looks at me and then at Harley.

Harley turns to me, obviously making a play to shift the

attention off of herself. "When do you think you and Sedona will have another?"

I shrug. "Let me get her to agree to move in with me first. We're on the baby step plan."

I hate that there's annoyance in my tone, but part of me feels as if Sedona's not one hundred percent in this. I get her reasoning for wanting to go slow, but we're doing great. What's slow going to accomplish except delaying us from ending exactly in the same spot, just way later?

"Well," Harley says. "I probably would've gone slow, but I got pregnant."

"Go figure," Kingston says.

Harley gut-punches him. "I wasn't trying to."

He bends over, coughing. "Damn, I feel bad if Rome pisses you off."

I high five her.

"I just keep pushing a little each day," I say.

"Nothing like a little pressure to get her to move in with you." Kingston rolls his eyes.

"I'm sure Harley has a great punch, but I promise it'll hurt more coming from me."

Kingston holds up his hands. "Since when can no one in this family take a joke?"

Some of the parents arrive to get their girls, so I head over to their huddle to wrap up practice. Palmer and Linus go play with Dion as I squat to talk to the girls.

"Okay, great job today. Now remember, we have our first game in a month. It'll be at the new facility indoors. Yer making such great progress, we'll be more than ready by then." I put my hand in and all the girls put their hands in too. "Let's go, Sharks!"

All the girls scream *Sharks*, their vote for our team

name. I've never felt prouder of them than today. The hard work they're putting in is starting to show.

The girls file out and one of the dads calls me over.

"Hey Jamison," he says. "I just had a quick question."

This dad always has a question. He has older sons who play, and he's either asking me to work with them or telling me how I should handle his daughter. In my short time of teaching kids, I've found that it's the parents who are the problem most of the time.

"What's up, Dave?"

"I just heard the news. Congratulations. But what happens now?"

"I'm sorry?" I tilt my head, hands on my waist, unsure what he's talking about.

"If you go off to be an assistant coach in the Premier League, what happens here? Is it an off-season thing? Or is Kingston taking over? Because I know he knows baseball but—"

I put up my hand. "What are you talking about?"

Then we're interrupted by Kingston yelling to me, holding out his cell phone. "*Jamie, it's Sedona!*"

I left mine in my bag, so she must have called him. I hold up my hand to tell Kingston to give me a minute.

"The coaching opportunity. You're on the shortlist. It's all over the sports channels. I didn't know you wanted back in the scene again after, well... you know." Dave shoves his hands in his pockets and rocks back on his feet as if he's embarrassed.

I hate that my past is up for public consumption.

"I'm not going anywhere," I say.

His eyebrows shoot up. "Well, according to the sports channels, you are."

Kingston comes closer, phone still in hand. "Jamie, she's demanding to talk to you."

"I promise you, Dave, I'm not going anywhere."

He blows out a breath. "Thank God. Just when I thought about asking you to give my boys a few lessons. We're lucky to have you here. I want to take advantage of the privilege." He claps me on the shoulder.

"Thanks."

After waving goodbye to Dave, Kingston hands me the cell phone. "I think she's upset."

"Where's Palmer?" I look behind me.

"She's with the other kids."

"You got her for me?"

He nods. "Yeah, go talk to Sedona. Something's wrong."

I rush toward my bag to pack up. There's no way she's heard about whatever Dave is talking about. It's not like she watches the sports channels. "Hey, lass, what's up?"

"How could you not tell me you've accepted a job halfway across the world?"

"Give me the phone!" Phoenix screams in the background.

"I would have understood. I never would've kept her from you. Is that what you thought? That I'd be some horrible ex who never let you see your kid?"

"What is going on? Where are you?" I grab my keys out of my pocket and look toward the field where Palmer is with Calista as Calista shows her how to stop a ball with the toe of her shoe. Palmer does it and falls. Calista is quick to help her up, and she signs to Palmer how to do it again. My heart melts from witnessing their bond forming.

"It's all over that you put your name in to be an assistant for Premier. How did you think I wouldn't find out? Were you just going to disappear on us? Do what I did to you as some sick joke?"

"Sedona, none of that is true. I'm not going to Premier. Where are you?"

There's a fumbling noise.

"We're not telling you that! Pack your bags and get the hell out of Lake Starlight," Phoenix screams and hangs up.

Fucking hell.

"King!" I yell.

He looks up from where he's playing with the ball with Dion. I sign for him to grab Palmer and take her home when he leaves, and he nods.

I dial Sedona and it goes right to voicemail.

How could she think I'd leave her? She's usually so secure. Even the Britani thing didn't throw her. I slide into my SUV and drive to her apartment, running through a red light.

After racing up the steps, I knock and hear nothing. Using the key she gave me two weeks ago, I open the door, but there's no sign of her.

I text the group thread I have going with her family to ask if anyone knows where she is. It sucks that they'll all know something is up, but Phoenix would've told them anyway. All I get is a stream of messages telling me they don't know where she is. The one who does would never tell me. Phoenix is probably loving this and talking me up as some monster to Sedona every minute that ticks by.

So I drive around Lake Starlight, hoping to find her SUV somewhere. An hour later, I'm back where I started. Until that same unknown number messages me.

Unknown number: *Check where you first met her. Bring a pie and two forks.*

Dori! How does she always know so much? I stop at Lard Have Mercy, buy a cherry pie, and ask for two disposable forks and napkins.

Then I'm out the door and driving to Lake Starlight High School. I walk around to the back of the school to the soccer pitch. Sure enough, Sedona's there, in the same bleachers she sat in all those years ago while she waited to interview me for the school paper.

I could kiss Dori right now.

THIRTY-TWO

Sedona

I told Phoenix to go home. I didn't want to listen to her told-you-so's anymore. Kingston messaged me to see if I was okay and let me know that he had Palmer because Jamison was out looking for me.

I decided to come here, where I first saw Jamison and his love for the game. His smile when he darted around Miles with the ball during that first game has never left my memory. Although I know he loves me, I've often wondered if he had to choose, which would be his number one? There was a time when he didn't have to choose, and he could have both. Now, he has to decide about not just me, but Palmer as well. And maybe it's Palmer keeping him here, not me.

I spot Jamison walking down the paved path to the bleachers in front of our old high school soccer field. His foot lands on the metal bleacher, and after the short climb, he sits next to me, putting a pie box from Lard Have Mercy next to him. We sit for a moment, neither of us saying a word.

Finally he says quietly, "I'm not going anywhere, Sedona."

"Then why does the news say differently?" I look in my lap, unable to meet his eyes. All my fears that I'm about to suffer a heartbreak bigger than I did before, make me feel raw and vulnerable.

"I guess word never got back that I wasn't interested. I swear no one has reached out to me. I would've told them if they did."

"Told them what?" I glance at him and he holds my gaze.

"Told them my life is in Lake Starlight with my girlfriend and our daughter."

"I think you should take the job if you can." I walk down the bleachers to the fence line. "Your heart is on that field."

He follows me, his footsteps so much louder than my own. "My heart is right here." He presses his hand to my chest. "My heart is always with you."

"You know, the first time I saw you here, you were this cocky new kid from Scotland. All the girls wanted to date you, and the guys wanted to be you. But all you cared about was playing the game. One thing I loved about you was how you loved something so fiercely. Witnessing you fulfill your dreams and get what you wanted after working so hard was amazing. I was always in awe of you, and I placed you on a pedestal for it."

"Yer wrong."

"About what? Soccer is your first love." He can't deny that. He's told me as much.

"Yer right on that. Soccer was my first love. But then my

parents signed me up to study abroad, and I showed up in this small town in Alaska and found my soulmate. Soccer was only my *first* love because I hadn't met you yet. Yer my *forever* love." He chuckles and straightens, staring at the field. "The first time I met you, Miles was talking about you in the locker room, saying how you wanted to interview me... I heard it in his voice."

"What?"

"He had feelings for you. He was threatened by me on the field and off."

My forehead scrunches. "What are you talking about?"

"I wanted to be a good teammate. I didn't want to take someone else's opportunity. But as arrogant as it sounds, I knew I was better than Miles. That his spot on the team was going to be mine. I figured I'd do the interview as a favor to him. That you'd be thankful and maybe date him."

"Why am I just hearing about this now?"

He continues on as if he didn't hear me. "When he introduced us, your gaze flowed down my body just like all the other girls. But the feeling of your eyes on my body was different. Then we shook hands and I didn't stand a chance. You sucked me in."

I give him my "yeah right" look. He's got to be kidding. I knew Miles flirted, but he didn't have a thing for me.

"Why do you think I suggested the diner? I could have done the interview during lunch. Or said to meet me after school one day I didn't have practice."

Maybe his attraction was instant like mine.

"I always felt horrible when we'd see Miles, but I couldn't stop myself from being around you. Then we fell in love. Everything just fit. You didn't care about me being the soccer hero. You cared about me, my hopes and dreams." He grabs my hand. "I know I lost my way a couple years ago and I put us in jeopardy. I know you think it showed you that I would pick soccer over you, but that's not the case. You win every time."

I nod. "I'm embarrassed that I assumed the news was telling the truth. But soccer is something I always felt I couldn't compete with."

He puts his finger under my chin and urges me to look at him. "I love you, Sedona. My life is here, and I don't want to be anywhere else. I know that's hard to believe after what you witnessed when my career ended, but I've found another purpose in life."

I walk into him, and he holds me against his firm chest while I hiccup out a sob. "I'm sorry."

He runs his hands down my back. "You have nothing to be sorry for. This is all new ground for us." He dips his head and kisses me lightly. "Move in with me."

My shoulders fall and I step away. "We've been over this, Jamie."

"Just hear me out." He climbs the bleachers, sits, and grabs the pie, opening the box and handing me a fork. "Have some pie while I work my case."

I follow him and sit. "You're sneaky, using the pie."

He places the cherry pie on my lap. The buttery crust does look mouth-watering. Then he stands at the bottom of the bleachers like a lawyer about to deliver his final argument. "You think that what's mine is ours, right? Technically, in this moment, Palmer isn't mine."

I look blankly at him and he chuckles.

"Her last name is Bailey, not Ferguson."

"We're changing that," I say.

"Yes, but she's yours only. Yet you share her with me."

"Pretty farfetched, Ferguson." I fork the pie, my heart

relieved because I jumped to conclusions and he's not leaving.

"So what if I have more money? It's our money. Because everything of mine, including my heart and body, are yours. They don't belong to me. That goes for my bank account too. Plus, how will either of us succeed if we don't tackle this parenthood thing together? What if yer working hard to get somewhere on an article and Palmer is there with constant interruptions? If we're together in the same house, I can keep her busy while you work. Take her to the facility with me or something."

I roll my eyes, but his argument makes sense. There have been so many times when I'm in the flow and I'm interrupted because Palmer needs something. Writing takes me at least twice as long as it ever did.

"During our lives, the role of breadwinner will probably flip and flop a bunch of times. What if you write some bestselling novel or your blog goes viral and everyone wants a piece of it? You could be the big earner between us." He sits on the bench in front of me and places his hands on the outsides of my thighs. "Would you not want to share that with me?"

Damn him, he really does have a good case.

"Point made," I say.

"So we can live together? You, me, and Palmer? Like a real family?"

I stare at him, the boy turned guy turned all man. How can I turn him down when I want the same things he does?

"Never let go of us again?" I say past the lump in my throat.

He takes the pie off my lap, places it next to me, then grabs my fork and puts it on the pie. Grabbing my hands in his, he squeezes. "I will never let you go again."

I exhale as if I'm preparing to jump off a cliff into the darkest and deepest water. But having Jamison jumping beside me with his hand in mine says we'll get through whatever life throws at us—together.

I nod.

His mouth crashes against mine and we make-out like teenagers—except we don't hide under the bleachers, we make-out in plain sight. Go ahead Buzz Wheel. Report that I got my man back. I want the entire world to know.

EPILOGUE

Sedona

One Month Later

Today is the official opening of Kingston and Jamison's youth sports facility. Palmer and I moved into Jamison's house last weekend, and since then, we've had a hard time getting Palmer away from her dollhouse.

While Palmer naps, I'm in the kitchen, working on a post about staycations in the Anchorage area. With Jamison having to stay around to get the facility open, we can't travel, and I'm not ready to leave them yet. It took having a family of my own for me to understand why my mom always took my dad with her.

I hear the door open, and since we're meeting Jamison later, I'm not sure who would just barge into my house. I realize my naivety when a blue-haired woman on a mission walks from the front door to my kitchen table.

"Hi, Grandma," I say. "What are you wearing?"

She's decked out in a long trench coat with the collar up covering half her face and a pair of Blue Blockers on.

"I didn't want anyone to recognize me."

I refrain from telling her that I'm pretty sure anyone who got within fifty feet of her would still know it's her.

She lays a laptop on the table. "Sedona, we need to talk."

I raise my eyebrows and shut my computer. She's serious as she slides out the chair and sits down. She's yet to ask where Palmer is, which is odd. "What's up?"

"Have I ever told you I hate that expression? All I think about is that damn rabbit with the carrot whenever I hear it."

I nod. I'm positive she didn't come all the way here to tell me that, but I change my wording to appease her. "What can I help you with?"

"Much better." She opens her computer, hunts and pecks with her pointer fingers, then turns the computer to face me. I'm shocked by the ease she seems to use with the laptop.

I lean forward, seeing the Buzz Wheel article that went live last night. It talks about Kingston and Jamison's facility and how they turned a vacant industrial building into an indoor sports complex. There's also a picture someone got of Jamison's parents with Palmer by the lakefront. They came to visit last week and instantly fell in love with their granddaughter. The last bit of the article talks about the rumor that Phoenix is pregnant, and it speculates on whether she and Griffin got married on the sly.

"Yeah, I saw it."

I'm not about to give her the intel she wants on Phoenix. Phoenix and Griffin *did* elope to Las Vegas last weekend while everyone else thought they were in LA. Maverick doesn't even know yet. She finally accepted his proposal and he booked his private plane immediately, saying he wasn't taking any chances. I'm disappointed I didn't get to be a part of the ceremony, but I'm glad she finally saw the light.

"No." Grandma Dori shakes her head and nudges the computer closer.

I see the headline, the article, but what I missed at first glance was that this is the Buzz Wheel website's *dashboard* —as in, the backend of the website where you load the posts. A smile fills my face. "Shut up. Really? You're Buzz Wheel?"

She nods, pride and resignation on her aging face.

"Why?" I ask.

"Because I had to know what was going on with each of you. I don't have eyes and ears everywhere. It was a good way for Lake Starlight as a whole, and a way to keep tabs on you all."

"You could have just asked us what's going on." I pull the computer closer, looking at all the archived articles she unpublished at midnight. There're years of gossip from this town sitting there.

"None of you ever would've told me. When your parents died, I knew it was up to me to make sure you all ended up happy and none of you ended up with dimwits. This seemed like a good way to do that. It meant everyone else was looking out for each of you, even when I couldn't. Soon people were obsessed with the Bailey kids getting their happily-ever-afters."

"Jeez, Grandma, why are you telling me this?" I slide through article after article.

"Because you're going to take it over now. I'm old, and I

want to enjoy my great-grandchildren now that you're all happy and in love."

"Me? But you could have picked anyone."

She pats my hand. "None of the others can write. Do what you want with this. Make it your own. I'm sure you youngsters know ways to make this profitable, if that's what you want to do."

My shoulders slouch. "Are you sure? I think people will miss your voice. I can't believe this entire time I never knew. I actually thought it was someone who hated us."

She laughs. "I tried to spin it sometimes."

"Wait. How did you set up this entire thing? No offense, you were a wonderful businesswoman, but you're not very tech-savvy."

"Well, Ira who used to work at Bailey Timber, his son is pretty good with computers. They live in Hawaii. I told him if he told anyone, I know people who could make him disappear. I'm not sure he was scared though. I think he's just a decent man." She pats my hand again. "So it's all yours now."

Tears well in my eyes that she'd trust me with such a huge thing.

"But you can't tell anyone." She points at me. "Not even Jamison."

"Um..."

"Fine, but only Jamison. That's your one confidant. I had Ethel, you have Jamison."

That makes me feel better. "Okay. Don't you worry that you'll be bored? Now that you're giving this up and we've all found our happily-ever-afters?"

She tsks and stands. I shut the computer, holding it out to her.

"I didn't say I'm going to stop meddling. You kids don't

know everything about life. I still have to offer my guidance and wisdom. Do you think marriage and raising children is easy? I have an entire arsenal of advice to give. Besides, I have a new mission." She pushes the computer back toward me. "It's yours now."

"Are you sure?"

She waves me off. "Just keep the thing."

I hug her, and she pats my back before stepping back. "Thanks for trusting me."

"Don't let your head get too big. I'll let you know if you're steering it wrong." She grins before heading to the front door. "Ethel's in the car. Did you hear the good news?"

"What?" I follow her.

"Calista's team is playing Ethel's grandson's team today." She stops at the door and lowers her voice. "The Baileys better kick their ass. I had Cleo make noisemakers and signs."

"Isn't it just a bunch of eight-year-olds?"

She stares at me as though she's wondering if we're related. "It's never too early to learn that second place is just the first loser."

I nod and purse my lips. "How did we turn out so normal?"

She opens the door, and just as fast as she came in, she's gone. Not even stopping to answer my question. Grandma Dori climbs into her Cadillac, and Ethel backs it up so fast she almost hits the mailbox.

I close the door and say a little thank you that Grandma Dori's part of our lives. Not a lot of grandparents would start a blog just to stay connected to their grandkids' lives.

I walk up the stairs and open Palmer's door. She's sitting

in her crib, playing with the plush mini soccer ball Jamison gave her when we moved in.

Good nap?

She nods and stands for me to get her out. When her feet hit the floor, she rushes over to her dollhouse, but I tap her on the shoulder.

She glances at me, and I sign, *Let's go. Daddy waiting.*

As if she forgot, Palmer charges toward the door, but I swoop her up and put her on the changing table. I pretend to tickle, and all she signs is *hurry* over and over again. It's rare I'm with her without Jamison nowadays, so I savor the moment. Oh, how our life has changed.

I'm not sure how long Jamison will wait to propose. The man has no pause button, but I'm learning that it's okay. Maybe his gut does lead him, but it kept bringing him back to me, so that's just fine.

A HALF-HOUR LATER, I pull up to the new facility. The parking lot is pretty full, and I take Palmer by the hand and walk up the sidewalk. Two guys are outside, talking.

"I told you the mix was shit," one of them says.

I look back at him and then at my daughter. He doesn't know she's deaf.

"Sorry, ma'am," the one says.

Ma'am I mouth to myself. Ouch. I think he's older than me.

"Let's just go back to the brewery after this game. I can't believe we all got guilted into coming here." The guy opens the door for Palmer and me.

"You know Grandma. She always gets what she wants," the other says, following right behind me.

"Isn't that the truth."

I feel a kinship with these guys. I assume they're Ethel's grandkids. Little do they know how much worse it could be.

Inside, all my siblings are present and accounted for. The kids and Cleo are handing out noisemakers.

I sit with Palmer on the bench.

Jamison runs over and kisses Palmer and me. "Wish us luck."

"Good luck, but you guys got this."

Cleo sits down next to me. "Doesn't this seem crazy? I mean, when I was eight, I was playing Barbies. Calista looks like a beast out there."

My gaze goes to the field, and sure enough, Calista's got eye black on under her eyes, her hair is in two braids, and there's a bandana around her head. "If Jamison gets his way, that's going to be Palmer in six years."

Cleo mindlessly runs her hands over her stomach but says nothing.

"You feel okay?" I ask.

She looks at me with a panicked expression. "Yep. Just something I ate."

I nod. "For a second, I thought you were pregnant."

She waves me off. "Denver would never keep that quiet."

Note to self, Cleo cannot lie. Her one eye is twitching. I think I just got my first gossip for Buzz Wheel tonight. Shit, I can't give away my family secrets. On the other hand, I need to keep Grandma Dori's legacy going.

"How far along?" I whisper.

"Eight weeks. Twins."

My mouth falls open. The money was on someone in our family having twins, and of course it's Denver. I hope for Cleo's sake, it's not two boys. That would be karma sticking it to Denver, but Cleo would be the collateral damage.

"Congratulations," I whisper, not making a big deal. "You and Harley and..."

"Phoenix," she says. I'm not surprised she told her, given that she's pregnant as well.

Damn this family. What is it with everyone getting pregnant at the same time?

Denver slides in next to Cleo. He grabs the plastic bottles with pieces of plastic and ribbons tied to it, shaking them over and over again. "It's starting."

Palmer bounces on my lap and claps.

"Go, Rylan!" a woman says from the bleachers next to us.

Denver stands. "Go, Calista!"

"Oh great, we're going to have a competition on who can be the loudest," Cleo mumbles.

Phoenix stomps on the bleachers, and the other family does the same.

The whistle is blown, and Calista gets the ball. She jets down the field. We're all cheering. Then a kid steals it from her and the other bleachers cheer.

It's easy to figure out Rylan is Ethel's grandson, Rylan Greene. He and Calista go back and forth, the two of them the best on their teams. At one point, Rylan accidentally trips Calista and I swear Kingston has to keep Denver and Rome from jumping onto the field. My attention is mostly on my man, who's running up and down the field with the girls, yelling out instructions and plays that they're actually following. When they have a break in the play, he gives high fives and tells the girls what a great job they're doing.

I kiss Palmer's head. We're so fortunate to have a man

like him in our lives. She claps and signs *Go Go* when Calista has the ball.

It's touch-and-go, and funny enough, after forty-five minutes, the game ends in a tie. Calista's team and the other all slap hands while we stand to leave.

Grandma stops us. "I want to introduce you all to Ethel's grandchildren."

As though Ethel told her grandkids the same thing, we end up lined across from one another. The Baileys on one side. The Greenes on the other. Through the introduction, I figure out that the two men from outside are Cade and Jed. Mandi, I recognize from the SunBay Inn. Other than that, the names are a blur. The only difference between us and them is they have no little ones. In fact, there are no plus ones at all in their group, which makes me think I need to move Buzz Wheel up to Sunrise Bay. My gut tells me that this is Dori and Ethel's next mission. Lord help the Greenes.

We all shake hands and say hello. It's polite and friendly, but awkward.

"Firstborn too?" Austin says to Cade.

Cade nods.

As though Austin has read my mind, he says, "Good luck to you."

Cade looks confused, and his gaze falls to his brother next to him like *what's this guy wishing me good luck for?* Us Baileys laugh as if we're in the know of an inside joke. Which we kind of are. We all say our goodbyes.

I'm walking with Palmer when a low voice says from behind me, "Excuse me, ma'am, but I'm going to have to frisk you." Jamison grabs Palmer and throws her in the air.

"If I get ma'amed one more time today, I'm gonna lose

it." I watch Cade and Jed walk past me, oblivious to the fact they ruined my day with one word.

"Don't worry, yer a definite MILF," Jamison says with Palmer still in his arms.

"I'm technically a SMILF," I say.

He's purposely not signing to Palmer and she grows agitated. She's cluing in on the fact she doesn't get sign language when it's something she shouldn't know.

"Yeah, I burned that shirt in the bonfire we had two days ago."

"What?" I screech a little too loudly and a few heads turn.

Calista runs over to us. *Hi, Palmer. I'm happy you came.*

"Yer not single," Jamison says.

I hold up my left hand. "Technically, I am."

We both look down to see Calista signing what we're saying.

Jamison hands her Palmer. "Go show her your moves."

Calista happily agrees, but they only get so far before they're stopped by Austin.

Jamison crosses his arms. "You know I'd ask you if I didn't think you'd strong-arm me."

"Who said I'd strong-arm you?"

He eyes me as though he's trying to read my thoughts. "I do wonder how you convinced your sister to accept a marriage proposal, but you won't take the same advice yourself?" He tilts his head, waiting for an answer.

"We could stand here and debate this subject, or you could sneak me into your office, and we could make-out."

He grabs my hand and tugs me, weaving through the throngs of people until we're secure in his office. "You said something about making out?"

I push him to the wall, and he stumbles until his back

hits it. Rising up on my tiptoes, I press my lips to his, but he's the one who places his hand on the back of my head, turning us so he can cage me against the wall. He locks me to the wall with his hips, and his thick length hits me in the stomach. Damn, I had him this morning and I could go again.

He slows the kiss, leaving me breathless and a little faint. "Marry me and I'll kiss you like that every day."

"I think you'll kiss me like that every day without me marrying you."

He chuckles and shakes his head. "You know me too well."

"I do. Thank you for admitting that." I lift on my tiptoes again. "But don't go thinking I would say no if you asked."

"If I ask you now and you say no, I'm going on a sex strike."

I giggle. "I'd like to see how long you'd last."

"Prepare yourself." He rounds the desk and fishes out a ring box. Falling to his knee, he opens it. "I had this whole thing planned with Palmer, but I think this moment is just for us to share. Like we didn't do it all out of order anyway. Although I'd change nothing. Well, that's not true."

I nod, knowing full well what he would change. I would change it too. We wouldn't have spent the first year and a half of Palmer's life apart. But that's behind us now.

"Sedona, will you make my dream come true and marry me?"

"Is this just so you can hang that Ferguson sign on the door?"

He shakes his head. "You caught me."

"You did pay good money for that sign. I suppose I should marry you then."

He waits for a real answer, so I fall to my knees and put my hands on his holding the ring box.

"I was thinking you could take my name though. Jamison Bailey has a great ring to it."

"Sedona," he says, clearly growing annoyed.

"Okay, I guess I'll be Mrs. Sedona Ferguson. If I must."

"You must." He doesn't wait to slide on the gorgeous round diamond, set on a platinum band, on my finger. "That never comes off."

I laugh and kiss him. "I love it, and I love you. Now for the wedding date."

I stand, and he kisses me again as though it's our last one for years. "Don't make me fly you to Las Vegas."

"No worries. Courthouse will do."

"Next week?" he asks.

I shrug. "Sure."

"Man, yer easy."

"Watch it."

He chuckles, then his lips are on mine and I'm nestled in his arms like the cherished treasure he's always treated me as.

After my parents died, I doubted whether my siblings and I could ever really be happy again. But time and community and family taught us all that we can. It doesn't mean that we don't miss our parents and wish they were here. But life moves on and we did our best to move on with it. In the end, life cannot get any sweeter than this moment. The one where you know the rest of your days will be surrounded by love.

The End

COCKAMAMIE UNICORN RAMBLINGS

Let's celebrate the fact that all the Bailey siblings are off and living their happily ever afters with the love of their lives! Yay!

Sedona is the one storyline that evolved from the beginning of the series, though most of it was off page and in our heads. When you read about Jamison and Sedona in book one, Lessons from a One-Night Stand, we weren't sure what was going to happen with them except that they would have to break up at one point. We threw around a lot of ideas early on. The original one being that their relationship would've ended in high school and they wouldn't have come back together until after college. Then as we wrote each Bailey book it was hard to get every character in at some point. We brought Jamison back in Phoenix's book, Confession from a Naughty Nanny, more for Phoenix rather than Sedona, but it fit perfectly. Writing a couple even as little as they appeared was hard knowing we had to break them up at some point. But there's this saying in writing called 'kill your darlings' and we knew at some point we'd have to do just that.

While writing the Bailey series, Piper had a vision of Jamison returning to Lake Starlight and Sedona being pregnant with someone else's baby. But this is before we ever decided that Sedona would be pregnant herself when she left Jamison. So we had to rework some timelines but we think it was all worth it in the end because it was a great twist and so very fitting for the Baileys.

While writing Juno and Colton in Secrets of the World's Worst Matchmaker, we finally hashed out Sedona and Jamison's storyline. And it was sad and heartbreaking but we knew these two were meant to be together. Even good people find themselves dealing with situations beyond their control sometimes and they don't do the best job of it. That's all part of life. But Jamison fought hard to be the man his lady love and daughter needed him to be which makes their HEA even sweeter in our minds.

And BuzzWheel... we know you aren't surprised it was Grandma Dori who wrote it. How could it be anyone else!?!

We're just going to reflect for a moment now on the series as a whole...

Almost two years ago, the two of us sat in a hotel room at a writing conference with our assistant, Shawna. We made a decision to write a nine book series not knowing the outcome. What if after three books, the series was bombing and we were committed to six more? We were scared to break away from our three book series formula. And now as we draw the series to an end, we're not ready to say goodbye. This family we love so much gained traction over the past two years, earning *USA Today* Bestseller status on book #7 and #8. Although we wanted that title, we only wanted it to be because that many readers were enjoying our stories. You've all loved and adored and championed this family these past couple of years and there are not enough thank you's we could give you to express how appreciative we are. THANK YOU!

And without our team listed below, these stories would never see the light of day!

Danielle Sanchez and the entire Wildfire Marketing Solutions team!

Cassie from Joy Editing for line edits.

Ellie from My Brother's Editor for line edits.

Shawna from Behind the Writer for proofreading.

Our sensitivity readers— Kristi Myers, Laura Anne, Kim Rust and Alyce Zawaba.

Sarah from Okay Creations for the cover and branding for the entire series.

Sara from Sara Eirew Photography for the awesome picture of Sedona and Jamison.

Bloggers who consistently carve out time to read, review and/or promote us.

Our Piper Rayne Unicorns who champion this series to others with their whole hearts.

You the reader who took a chance on our book with so many choices out there!

No tears! No tears! Operation Bailey Birthday is coming in November and someone is having a very special birthday and we're going to fast forward in time a bit! So no tears until the candles are blown out!

XO,
    Piper & Rayne

ABOUT PIPER & RAYNE

Piper Rayne is a USA Today Bestselling Author duo who write "heartwarming humor with a side of sizzle" about families, whether that be blood or found. They both have e-readers full of one-clickable books, they're married to husbands who drive them to drink, and they're both chauffeurs to their kids. Most of all, they love hot heroes and quirky heroines who make them laugh, and they hope you do, too!

ALSO BY PIPER RAYNE

The Baileys

Lessons from a One-Night Stand

Advice from a Jilted Bride

Birth of a Baby Daddy

Operation Bailey Wedding (Novella)

Falling for My Brother's Best Friend

Demise of a Self-Centered Playboy

Confessions of a Naughty Nanny

Operation Bailey Babies (Novella)

Secrets of the World's Worst Matchmaker

Winning My Best Friend's Girl

Rules for Dating your Ex

Operation Bailey Birthday (Novella)

The Greenes

My Twist of Fortune (FREE)

My Beautiful Neighbor

My Almost Ex

My Vegas Groom

The Greene Family Summer Bash

My Sister's Flirty Friend

My Unexpected Surprise

My Famous Frenemy

The Greene Family Vacation

My Scorned Best Friend

My Fake Fiancé

My Brother's Forbidden Friend

The Modern Love World

Charmed by the Bartender

Hooked by the Boxer

Mad about the Banker

Complete Set (all 3 books)

The Single Dad's Club

Real Deal

Dirty Talker

Sexy Beast

Complete Set (all 3 books)

Hollywood Hearts

Mister Mom

Animal Attraction

Domestic Bliss

Bedroom Games

Cold as Ice

On Thin Ice

Break the Ice

Complete Set (all 3 books +)

Charity Case

Manic Monday

Afternoon Delight

Happy Hour

Complete Set (all 3 books)

Blue Collar Brothers

Flirting with Fire

Crushing on the Cop

Engaged to the EMT

Complete Set (All 3 books)

White Collar Brothers

Sexy Filthy Boss

Dirty Flirty Enemy

Wild Steamy Hook-up

The Rooftop Crew

My Bestie's Ex

A Royal Mistake

The Rival Roomies

Our Star-Crossed Kiss

The Do-Over

A Co-Workers Crush

Hockey Hotties

Countdown to a Kiss (Free Novella)

My Lucky #13

The Trouble with #9

Faking it with #41

Sneaking around with #34

Second Shot with #76

Offside with #55

Printed in France by Amazon
Brétigny-sur-Orge, FR